'There's something in there. I can see something white.' Simon spoke in a dry whisper and Tan knew he was scared.

'What is it?' he asked. 'That old ghost again? Maybe he'll have a go at this wire if we ask him nicely.' He chuckled, hoping to joke Simon out of his fear. It didn't work.

'It's white, and it's not moving, and I can see it better now,' whispered the frightened boy. Tan screwed up his eyes, peering in the same direction. There was something. He could see it himself. Up against the wall of the tunnel, maybe fifteen metres away. Something white, which didn't move. He swallowed hard . . .

www.booksattransworld.co.uk/childrens

Also available by Robert Swindells, and
published by Corgi Yearling Books:

ABOMINATION
HYDRA
INSIDE THE WORM
INVISIBLE!
JACQUELINE HYDE
NIGHTMARE STAIRS
ROOM 13
TIMESNATCH

Published in hardcover, by Doubleday:

A WISH FOR WINGS

THE THOUSAND EYES
OF NIGHT

Written + illustrated
by Marina
          McKimm

ROBERT SWINDELLS

The Thousand Eyes of Night

CORGI YEARLING BOOKS

THE THOUSAND EYES OF NIGHT
A CORGI YEARLING BOOK : 0 440 864259

First published in Great Britain by
Hodder & Stoughton Children's Books, 1985

PRINTING HISTORY
Corgi Yearling edition published 1993
Reissued 2001

3 5 7 9 10 8 6 4 2

Set in 14/16 pt Linotype Century Schoolbook by
Chippendale Type, Otley, West Yorkshire

Corgi Books are published by Transworld Publishers,
61– 63 Uxbridge Road, London W5 5SA,
a division of The Random House Group Ltd,
in Australia by Random House Australia (Pty) Ltd,
20 Alfred Street, Milsons Point, Sydney, NSW 2061, Australia,
in New Zealand by Random House New Zealand Ltd,
18 Poland Road, Glenfield, Auckland 10, New Zealand
and in South Africa by Random House (Pty) Ltd,
Endulini, 5a Jubilee Road, Parktown 2193, South Africa.

Printed and bound in Great Britain by
Cox & Wyman Ltd, Reading, Berkshire

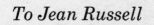

To Jean Russell

1

Twelve planets orbit Betelgeuse in Orion, where once there were thirteen. The thirteenth planet collided long ago with a dead comet and is stardust. The doomed world was home to the only intelligent life-form in the system. Seeing the collision coming, and being concerned to preserve what it thought of as its civilization, this life-form built and launched a swarm of projectiles: a cloud of tiny arks which fanned out across the void, carrying their deep-frozen passengers to new worlds, or to death ...

'G'night, you lot!' Tan Hanley hooked the padlock through the hasp and locked the shed. He'd fed the fourteen gerbils inside and tucked them up for the night. He could go in now and watch *Top of the Pops.*

He shivered. A thin November wind whipped across the garden, rattling the bare twigs of the sycamore. It could easily snow tonight, except that the sky was clear. He stood with his

9

shoulders hunched and his hands deep in his pockets, looking up. The stars were cold, hard spangles casting a faint radiance on the house-tops. He blew out a plume of breath and moved towards the house. As he did so a brief slash of silver split the sky. He saw it with the tail of his eye, and before he could turn his head it was gone. He stood for a moment, then shrugged and went on.

Falling star. You were supposed to make a wish but you'd have to be quick. Send me a million pounds. Turn Gary Deacon into a frog. Did it work, once the star had gone out?

He let himself in, locked the door and walked through the kitchen and along the hallway to the living room. His mother and sister were watching the end of *Look North*. He flung himself into an armchair and began to untie his shoelaces.

'Where's Dad?'

His mother glanced at him, smiling faintly. 'Upstairs, getting ready to go out. You know he can't stand *Top of the Pops*.'

'Huh!' scoffed Tan. 'Don't start blaming *Top of the Pops* for Dad going down the club. He goes on Fridays too remember, and it's not on then!'

Anne shot her mother an irritated look. 'Don't argue with him, Mum: once he starts he never knows when to stop.'

Tan would have offered some retort, but the *Top of the Pops* signature-tune burst into the room. 'I saw a falling star just now,' he said, to nobody in particular.

'Really?' His mother's voice was vague. 'They're lucky, you know.'

'Huh! Why aren't we millionaires, then?' He put his shoes beside the chair and reached for the old sandals he wore in the house.

Anne scowled, without taking her eyes from the screen. 'Shut up, you two: it's them.'

'Ooo wow!' squealed Tan. 'She fancies him you know, Mum: that one there in the middle. Don't blame her either: he's a damned-sight better looking than that Tim she's knocking around with. Now if you were going out with *him* . . . '

'Tan!' reproved his mother. 'Your sister's trying to listen, and she's not knocking around with anybody. Anne doesn't knock around, whatever that means. And Tim Bixby's a very nice boy. I'd like to think . . . '

'If you don't know what it means, how d'you know she's not doing it?' He was fed up of hearing about Tim rotten Bixby. Pilot Officer Bixby. Pilot Officer! He wasn't a pilot at all. He worked in the next office to Mum, up at the camp. He must be pretty desperate, too, thought Tan savagely, to be going out with Anne. He was about to say something to that effect when his sister shot out of the sofa and ran from the room.

'Now see what you've done,' said his mother. 'You know she likes that group. She's been looking forward to this all day and now you've spoilt

11

it for her.' From upstairs came the sound of a door slamming.

'Me?' cried Tan indignantly. 'What did I do? All I said was ...'

'Tristan!' Tan groaned softly to himself. His father had come down and was in the doorway, knotting his tie. 'What have you been saying to Anne? She's just rushed past me in tears and slammed her bedroom door. You know she's at a difficult age, and yet you persist in teasing her.' He finished his tie and reached for the jacket that hung from the back of a chair. 'Whatever it was, you'd better go up and apologize. There's enough trouble in the world without a lot of silly fratching between brother and sister.'

Tan assumed a resigned expression and got to his feet. 'All I said was ...'

'Never you mind. Just go upstairs and apologize, Tristan. All right?'

'Yes, Dad.'

He left the room and started to climb the stairs. It was cold out here. He could hear Anne blubbering in her room. What's she got to cry about? he asked himself. Difficult age! I wish I was seventeen and she was twelve, instead of the other way round. They always side with her, and it's going to take more than a falling star to alter my rotten luck. He sighed, and knocked softly on his sister's door.

2

At breaktime next morning, Tan mentioned the falling star to his friend Simon. 'It was pretty close,' he said. 'I reckon it could have come down on the Tangle. How about us having a look for it tomorrow?'

Simon shrugged and pulled a face. He was one of those boys who reads a lot and seems to know everything about everything. 'It won't have come down on the Tangle,' he said. 'It won't have come down at all. They burn up when they hit the Earth's atmosphere.'

'Big-head!' growled Tan. 'They do come down sometimes though: I've seen pictures of them. Meteorites. They're made of metal.'

'Yes,' replied Simon. 'Sometimes. Very rarely. When one does reach the ground in one piece, it's in the papers.'

'And this could be one of them,' Tan persisted.

'It could be,' admitted Simon, 'but I doubt it. Anyway, we'll be on the Tangle whether or not: we always are, so we can have a look round if it'll make you happy.'

'Thanks a lot!' said Tan, sarcastically. 'Simon Playfair: the Patrick Moore of Market Fulford County Primary.'

'Drop dead!'

Saturday morning was cold and misty. His dad was needed at the canning plant, so Tan had to go with his mother to the supermarket. It was after eleven when he made his way through the quiet streets towards the place they called the Tangle. The Tangle was a long, narrow stretch of derelict land that had once been a railway station. The station had closed down before Tan was born. Its buildings had been pulled down, and now the place was a wilderness of weeds, waist-high grass and heaps of smashed masonry. People came at night and dumped mattresses and old prams on it, and everybody's parents hated their children playing there. They played there anyway, though, because it was easily the best place in Market Fulford for playing on. The only bit nobody was keen on was the tunnel that yawned blackly at one end. Just before the station closed, a porter had committed suicide by lying down in the tunnel and letting the four-fifteen from Crewe trundle over him, and now his ghost was thought to haunt the spot. Now and then, for a dare, somebody would venture a little way into the cold, sooty darkness, but nobody, not even Gary Deacon and his gang, went in very far, nor lingered very long.

When Tan reached the Tangle, Simon and Diane were already there. They were by the gap in the dilapidated fence, looking for him. Diane was Simon's sister. She was a year younger than the boys, and had once gone so far into the tunnel, alone, that the knot of squealing children at its mouth had lost sight of her. She was all right, old Diane: everybody said so.

'Where the heck have you been?' demanded Simon. 'We've been here since eight. It was flipping freezing!'

'Sorry. I got caught for shopping. Have you found that meteorite?'

'No! I told you: they don't get down. We found a plastic horse though, and a pair of mossy trousers. D'you want to see?'

'Not really,' said Tan, gloomily. 'Any sign of the Deacon gang?'

'No, thank God. I reckon those trousers are Deacon's. He keeps 'em here for Sundays.' They laughed, but it was a nervous sort of mirth. Gary Deacon was fourteen and had about twenty kids in his gang. They regarded the Tangle as their territory, and did unpleasant things to anybody they caught on it. When you were playing on the Tangle you kept a sharp look out. It was the one drawback to the place.

'Let's have another look for that meteorite,' suggested Diane. 'Three pairs of eyes are better than two.'

'OK,' agreed Simon. 'There's nothing else to do anyway. Come on, Tan.'

They began wading through the long brown grass, peering down and turning bits of rubbish with their toes. It was cold, even though a watery sun was doing its best to break through the mist. Heads down, hands in pockets, they worked their way along the Tangle until they reached the area of hard-packed shale that lay before the tunnel. There was no need to search here: the ground was flat and almost bare. If anything had fallen on to it they would have seen it at once. There was only a rusty old tin, which Tan kicked, so that it slammed against the mouldering brickwork. He hadn't really expected to find anything, but there had been the million-to-one chance.

'Now don't get vicious,' railed Simon, 'just because I was right!'

'Shut it, Einstein,' growled Tan. Diane had approached the tunnel and was standing in its mouth, peering in. The boys sauntered up to her. 'What's up, Sis?' said Simon. 'Seen the headless phantom, have you?'

'I saw something,' she replied, tersely. Simon laughed, and the echo of it went skipping away into the blackness.

'Sssh!' She gripped her brother's sleeve. Tan glanced at her face and saw she wasn't pretending. 'Belt up, Simon!' he hissed. 'What was it, Diane?'

'I don't know. It was – whitish. I only saw it for a second. It was a long way in. When I looked at it, it went farther in and vanished.'

'How big was it?' Tan whispered. The girl levelled her palms, one above the other. 'About this high.'

Simon laughed again. 'Not big enough for a porter,' he said. 'Even without a head. You're seeing things, Sis: you're a nut-case.'

'Leave her alone, Simon,' growled Tan. He liked his friend's sister a lot better than his own. Besides, you could tell she was scared. 'All you can do is laugh at people. Why don't you go in there, if you think it's funny?'

'All right!' Simon started forward, a swagger in his step. 'No!' Diane darted forward, grabbed her brother by the sleeve of his anorak and tried to wrestle him back. 'Don't, Simon. I did see something, honestly. I don't want you to go in.'

For a moment he fought against her, then relaxed, chuckling. 'All right, Sis. All right. I won't go in, OK? I just wanted to show Tan there I'm not scared. I'm not, you know!' He put an affectionate arm round his sister's waist and walked with her, out into the weak sunshine. He screwed up his eyes, looking at Tan. 'What about you, Tan? Are you off in?'

'No he's not!' cried Diane, breaking away from him. 'Nobody's going in. I don't like it here. There's a – feeling about it: a

17

spooky feeling, as though something awful's going to happen. I think we should play somewhere else, like the park.'

'Boring!' scoffed Simon. 'The slide'll be wet and they've taken the swings down for the winter. How about it, Tan: do we go to the park?'

Tan hacked at the shale with the toe of his shoe. 'I don't care where we go. I'm not off in that tunnel because Diane's right: there is a funny feeling about it. Maybe it's Deacon and his mob, or maybe there is a ghost. Whatever it is, I don't feel like hanging around.'

In truth, Simon felt it too, though he pretended he didn't, and so they mooched off through the weeds, kicking things and chuntering to one another in subdued tones. They didn't know it, but it was to be their last visit to the Tangle for some time.

Snow fell heavily during the first week of December. Biting easterly winds blew it in great drifts across the Tangle until even the waist-high willow herb vanished beneath it. The clouds parted, and there followed a succession of bright, frosty nights which laid a brittle crust upon the snow.

Few ventured out on the Tangle. Those who did soon found themselves floundering and turned back with their gumboots full of melted snow, leaving half-circles of deep holes like bites to mark their passage.

Tan, Diane and Simon steered clear of the place altogether. The Playfairs had a four-man toboggan which they dragged out at the first fall, and the three friends spent all their free time riding it down steep, cobbled streets and dragging it back to the top.

The thaw came in the middle of the month and Market Fulford had what Simon called a brown Christmas. Every open space became

19

a quagmire. Toboggans were stowed away, icy rain lashed the town's windows and television came into its own.

January brought further snow and February froze through to the middle of March, to give the nastiest winter anybody could remember. By the time the Tangle dried out in April it had been virtually inaccessible for four months. During that time, something had begun there which was to bring Market Fulford and the world to the brink of disaster.

Half-past three, the first Wednesday in April. School had broken up for Easter, and the road was thronged with shrill children, excited at the prospect of a fortnight's freedom. Tan and Simon strolled along in the weak sunshine, making plans.

'We've got the rest of this week,' said Simon. 'Up to Saturday night, then we're away for a week, worst luck. Are you all right for looking after the guinea-pigs till we get back?'

Tan nodded gloomily. 'I suppose so. What d'you have to go away for: where you going?' Simon pulled a face. 'Our gran's near Birmingham. Rotten place: nowhere decent to play. She's Dad's mum. Knits all the time and talks about how terrific everything was when Dad was a boy. I wouldn't go, only Mum thinks I'm too young to be left alone at home, and Dad says Gran likes to see me.'

'Great. What does Diane reckon?' Diane was somewhere in front of them, walking with a gang of girls. Simon shrugged. 'I dunno. I think she'd rather stay at home too. It was all right when we were small: we liked going then, but it's pretty boring now. Aren't you off anywhere?'

Tan shook his head. 'Dad's working, except Good Friday and Easter Monday, and he says the roads are too busy to set off anywhere then.'

'You're lucky, then.'

'Huh!' Tan kicked a pebble. 'I'd be lucky if you were here, but it's not much fun on your own. Imagine being on the Tangle by yourself, and Deacon comes along. Bang! I'll probably end up hanging about at home, washing up and getting sent to the shops. I can't wait.'

'There's always Anne.'

'Yeah,' grunted Tan. 'Always. She's no good, you nit. She's seventeen and going out with this officer. Takes her all her time to talk to me. Here: d'you fancy a look at the Tangle?'

They had come to where the rotting fence divided the wilderness from the road. In some places it leaned drunkenly out over the pavement. Elsewhere it sagged inwards, or had disappeared entirely. Simon peered through a gap.

'Why not?' he said. 'It'll be pretty dry by now, I reckon.' It would be their first visit to the place since their retreat of the previous autumn.

They slipped through the gap and began picking their way down the shallow slope. Winter had flattened the weeds and grasses, which formed a brown sodden mat underfoot. Green blades were beginning to thrust their way through this mat and clumps of coltsfoot made brilliant splashes of gold among the rubble.

The two boys reached the flat bottom and turned right, moving in the direction of the tunnel. Tan recalled the strange fear which had overwhelmed him when last he was here, but time had blurred it so that now, in the spring sunshine, he wondered how he could have been so daft. He glanced over at his friend.

'Hey Simon: remember last time?' Simon had stopped and was peering at something on the ground. He nodded. ''Course I remember. Here: come and look at this.' Tan walked over. At Simon's feet lay the skeleton of a small animal. The bones were unscattered and lay among root-clumps in a flat, perfect pattern. He felt a stirring of unease and whispered, 'What is it?'

Simon looked at him. 'Cat. Must have been here most of the winter. I wonder whose it was?'

Tan shrugged. 'I dunno. They'll have given it up by now, anyway. Come on.' He moved on and Simon said, 'I'm having the skull for my collection.'

'Ugh!' Tan shivered. 'You're welcome. I wouldn't touch it with a ten-foot pole.'

'What's up with you all of a sudden?' Simon took a tissue from his pocket, wrapped up the skull and put it carefully into his anorak. 'You were dead chuffed when we found that rabbit

23

skeleton last sumer. We nearly had a fight over which of us was to have its skull.'

'I know. I let you have it though, and you can have that one, too. Come on.'

They continued towards the tunnel. A moment later Simon turned aside and poked at something with his foot. 'Deacon's pants are still here,' he announced. 'He must have worn his old ones all winter.'

Deacon! Tan glanced quickly all around. Two boys had followed them through the fence and were walking down the slope. Neither of them was Deacon. He looked at his watch. The upper school finished at a quarter to four. It was twenty-to.

'Come on, Simon,' he said. 'Big school's out in five minutes. I've got a feeling old Deacon'll drop in here on his way home, so if we're going to look at the tunnel let's do it and get out of here.'

There was nothing much to see. Somebody had dropped a mattress over the parapet. It lay at the mouth of the tunnel, its stained fabric already turning green. The two boys walked round it with their hands in their pockets. 'Good old Deacon,' said Simon. 'First he starts keeping his clothes here, and now he moves his bed in.' He gave the thing a kick, then bent forward with an exclamation.

'Hey, Tan: come here!'

'Not again!' Tan consulted his watch. 'If it's another skull you're welcome to it. I'm off.'

'It's not: it's a mouse.' Simon squatted down and plucked at a flap of torn material. 'There's loads of 'em in here: babies. A whole nest. Look!'

Tan came and squatted beside his friend. There was a hole in the side of the mattress. He saw a lot of fluffy grey stuff and some springs. Between two springs, on a nest of grey fluff, lay a clutch of young mice.

'Wow! I thought you were kidding, Simon. Get one out.' Simon put his hand into the hole, felt about and withdrew it. He placed the tiny creature on his palm. It ran, and Simon curled his fingers, holding it gently. The mouse darted its head about, looking at its captors with sharp, pink eyes. Its whiskers quivered. The boys' gazed at it.

'It's white,' breathed Tan.

'Yes.'

'I thought wild ones were grey, or brown?'

Simon nodded. 'They are. These must belong to a tame one that's escaped. I wonder where she is?'

'Dunno.' Tan reached out and stroked the little head with his finger. 'Maybe she's deserted 'em. She will anyway, now that we've put our scent on them.'

'I know,' said Simon. 'What shall we do?' He knew what he wanted to do, but he wasn't sure it was right. Still, if the mother deserted them . . .

'We'd better take them,' said Tan. 'They'll only starve if we don't. How many are there?'

'I don't know,' said Simon. 'Hang on.' He passed the mouse to his friend and put his hand into the hole again. By the time the nest was empty, they had five mice between them. They were quite lively, and it wasn't easy to prevent any escaping. Tan knelt on the wet ground and made an enclosure of his arms while Simon went and searched the long, dead grass for some sort of container. The other two boys were approaching and Tan wanted to be away before they got in on the act. He was worrying about Deacon, too. Simon came back with a plastic box that had once contained margarine. It had no lid, but the plastic was smooth and the little mice couldn't climb out. Simon undid his anorak and carried the box inside. They began hurrying away, passing the other boys. One of them said, 'What you got there?'

'Dead cat,' said Simon, proudly. 'Been dead months I should think: want to see?' He made as if to open his coat.

'Yuk!' cried the boy. 'No thanks. What the heck d'you want a dead cat for anyway?'

'Tea,' said Simon. 'See you!' They strode on down the Tangle, Simon peering under his anorak now and then to satisfy himself that all five mice were still there. They didn't pause till they were through the fence and across the road. Then Simon stopped and leaned on somebody's garden wall.

'Phew!' he gasped. 'I'm sweating like a pig. No sign of Deacon, though. How many of these do you want?'

'Well,' Tan replied, 'you found them, so you take three and I'll have the other two. You can give one of yours to Diane.'

'Yes: and you can give one of yours to Anne!'

'You must be joking: she'd pass out or something. Have you a spare cage?'

'Yes. Have you?'

'Yes. I suppose mice eat gerbil food, don't they?'

Simon nodded. 'Mice eat anything. We'll go by your place and drop yours off then. You out tonight?'

'I think so. I'll come for you. Seven all right?'

'Fine. Come on, then.' They went on, turning left into Cobden Street, and their shadows went before them.

5

'Simon's going away on Saturday,' said Tan, pushing a bit of tomato about with his fork. He was leading up to telling his parents about the mice. Gerbils were all right. Gerbils were clean, his mother always said. He wasn't at all sure she'd say the same for mice. She glanced up from her plate.

'Where's he going, Tan?'

'His gran's, near Birmingham.'

'By himself?'

'No. They're all going: the whole family.'

'Must be nice, that,' grunted his father.

'No,' Tan replied. 'He doesn't want to go.'

Mr Hanley shook his head. 'I don't mean that. I mean, it must be nice having a job like Playfair's. Lecturing. Same holidays as the kids. Longer sometimes.' Tan's dad worked at the cannery. Viners. He was Dispatch Manager, in charge of a fleet of trucks. It was an important job but the holidays weren't very good.

'Oh,' said Tan. 'Yes. I wish Mr Playfair worked at Viners, then I'd have Simon around all the holidays.'

'Selfish little beast!' snapped Anne. 'Always thinking about yourself.'

'Not always,' Tan flared. 'When I see the back-end of a pony I think about you.'

'Tristan!' His mother glared at him over a loaded fork. 'That's not very nice, is it? Where on earth did you pick up such a vulgar expression?'

He was about to reply when his father interrupted. 'Wherever he heard it,' he said, as though Tan wasn't there, 'he'd better not let me hear him use it again. There's many a lad would give his left arm to have a sister like Anne. He's forgotten how she used to stick up for him when he was small, that's his trouble!'

'No I haven't,' contradicted Tan. 'And I haven't forgotten how she used to torture me, either. She was like something out of the Gestapo with her skipping-rope and her Indian-burns. Can I leave the table?' he added. 'I don't want pudding.' He'd blown it: he knew that. He couldn't possibly bring up the subject of the mice now. Why was it, he wondered, that every time he opened his mouth around here he put his foot in it?

'Yes, Tan,' said his father, quietly. 'You may leave the table. In fact, I think you'd better. And if you were thinking of going out tonight, you can forget it. You have your animals to see to, and when you've finished doing that, and

29

have washed your hands thoroughly, you can relieve your mother and sister of the washing-up. Do I make myself clear?'

'Yes, Dad.' It was no use arguing. Positively dangerous in fact. He rose and left the room. He put his shoes on in the kitchen, let himself out and trailed miserably down the garden, muttering to himself.

What a terrific start to the holidays. No Simon next week, a row with his family and no playing out tonight. And on top of that, he'd landed himself with a load of washing-up. He sighed as he undid the padlock and let himself into the shed.

The shed had one small window which was covered with dust and spider-webs on the inside and streaks of dirt on the outside. It filtered the light, so that inside the shed it was dim, even in the middle of the day. Tan liked it like that. It was his own place: a place he could come to when he felt like being by himself. Nobody else came here, except Dad now and then for a spade or a hoe. His mother didn't mind gerbils but she wasn't crazy about them either, and Anne was terrified.

He pulled the door to behind him and breathed in. The warm air smelled of sawdust and bran. It made him feel better. He sighed again and grinned. Nuts to the lot of 'em, he thought. He'd give the three big cages a really thorough clean-out, then see to the mice. He'd popped

them into the spare cage without bedding or
anything. He bent down and peered through
the wire but he couldn't see them. They must
be in the sleeping compartment.

He was moving over to the big cages when
he became aware that something was wrong.
There was something different about the shed
tonight. What was it?

He paused, listening. Everything was quiet.
That's it, he thought: it's too quiet. Usually
when he came in the gerbils ran about, or
stood on their hind legs with their hands on
the wire and their noses through. He always
came at the same time and they'd got used to
it. They knew they were about to be fed.

Now there was nothing. No rustling of wood-
shavings: no bright eyes at the wire. Suddenly
afraid, he twisted the door-catch of the near-
est cage and looked in. The five animals sat
huddled together, watching him through frightened eyes.

He checked the other cages and stood with
his hand on the open door of the third one,
gazing in. They all looked scared to death –
even Action, Tan's favourite, who ran and leapt
and was afraid of nothing. He bent, peering
into the dim compartment and talking softly
to his pets.

'What is it, eh?' he crooned. 'Whatsa matter
– have we had a rat in here or something?' He
put out a hand and began stroking their silky

coats. The animals lifted their heads to nuzzle his finger, but they wouldn't stir otherwise. He scooped up Action and tried to lift her out, but the little creature jumped out of his palm and hid itself among the others. The animals were clearly terrified of something and Tan didn't persist. He closed the door gently and stood, a puzzled frown on his face.

Could they be frightened of the mice? he thought. Maybe I ought to release them. He didn't want to. They're only mice, he told himself. They can't do gerbils any harm, and anyway they're in a cage. We'll give it a day or two and see what happens. Then, if the gerbils are still nervous I'll take them back to the Tangle. He'd already decided to postpone the cleaning till tomorrow.

He got a scoop of sawdust and a handful of shavings and opened the spare cage. The two mice huddled in a corner, watching him. 'It's OK,' he murmured. 'Nobody's going to hurt you. Here.'

He inserted the scoop and sprinkled sawdust on the floor of the sleeping compartment. The mice separated and darted through into the main section, where they went into a huddle again. Tan chuckled. 'Not you two as well,' he whispered. 'What the heck's up with everybody tonight?'

He withdrew the scoop, thrust the ball of shavings into the compartment and put his face close to the wire. 'There you are,' he said. 'Plenty of nice warm bedding. Better than that smelly old mattress. And here's some supper too.' He took a handful of mixed cereal and dribbled it through the wire. 'Didn't get this sort of service on the Tangle, did you?' The two mice watched, but didn't come to the food. Tan pulled a face. 'All right,' he said. 'Suit yourselves, only don't say I didn't try.'

He topped up the gerbils' dishes, put fresh water in all the bottles and opened the shed door. 'G'night you lot,' he whispered into the quiet dimness. Nothing stirred. He shrugged, closed the door and locked up. Things might have simmered down in the house by now. If so, he'd ask Mum if he could phone Simon before washing up.

He crossed to the house. There was a stack of dirty dishes on the drainer. He walked through. His mother was tidying the living room. When she saw him she said, 'Do the washing-up, Tan love; Tim's calling for Anne at seven and we don't want a mess.'

'OK, Mum.' He'd known Tim must be coming by the way she was fussing around but he didn't say anything. He was in enough trouble as it was and besides, he needed to make that phone call.

'Can I use the phone first, Mum?' he asked. 'It won't take a minute, only Simon'll be hanging around waiting for me.' His mother nodded.

'Yes, Tan. You may use the phone, but you're not to spend half-an-hour chatting, d'you hear?'

He went out into the hallway and dialled. While he was waiting for someone to pick up the phone at the other end his father walked through, casting meaningful glances first at Tan, then back towards the kitchen. Tan nodded and flashed him a quick grin, which was not returned. Somebody picked up the phone.

'Hello?' said Tan. 'May I speak to Simon, please?'

'I'm sorry,' said Mrs Playfair. 'Simon went out ten minutes ago. It's Tan, isn't it?'

'Yes. I was supposed to be coming for him at seven.' He glanced at his watch. It was twenty past six. 'Did he say when he'd be back?'

'I'm afraid not, Tan. As a matter of fact he looked rather sheepish when he left. He was carrying a little box and didn't answer when I asked what was in it. You two haven't been doing something you shouldn't, have you?' She sounded anxious.

'No, Mrs Playfair.' He thought he knew what Simon had had in the box but he wasn't going to say so. The little creep had chickened out of telling his parents about the mice, and was getting rid of them.

'I rang to say I can't come anyway,' he continued. 'Will you tell him I'll see him on the – at the end of Cobden Street in the morning?'

'I'll tell him, Tan,' said Mrs Playfair. 'But you will stay away from that dreadful place you call the Tangle, won't you?' Her voice was tinged with irony and he knew she'd noticed his slip.

'We'll probably be going in the park, Mrs Playfair,' he said. It wasn't a lie. They probably would be, for a minute or two.

'Good. I'll see that Simon gets your message, Tan. Was there anything else?'

'No, nothing else, Mrs Playfair.'

'Goodbye then, Tan: thank you for ringing.'

''Bye.'

He replaced the receiver and went into the kitchen. He was angry with Simon. Why couldn't he have waited till Tan arrived and given the creatures to him? He was certain his friend had been carrying the mice in that box. He ran hot water into the sink, squirted in some green liquid and swished it about till the sink was a mass of suds. He scooped up a handful of these and blew them at the window but then he heard his father coming downstairs and began to do the dishes. He worked mechanically, his mind on Simon and the mice.

When the job was done he wandered through to the living room. His parents were watching TV. 'Finished, love?' said his mother, her eyes on the screen.

'Yes.' He sat down. The room was spick and span. Even his parents looked as though they'd been dusted and put back.

'Stacked everything away, have you?' asked his father.

'Yes, Dad.'

'And rinsed out the sink?'

Tan risked a sigh. 'Yes, Dad. It's like Buckingham Palace in there.'

'Good. This young man won't be accustomed to untidiness, you know.'

'Why do they say officer's mess, then?'

He ought not to have said it. Not tonight. He braced himself for the explosion but it never came. His father gave him a withering look and spoke quietly. 'Very funny, lad,' he said. 'I don't know why we bother with TV when we've got you in the house. We could all sit round you and save the licence fee.'

Tan, amazed at his escape, made no reply. Maybe shouting raised too much dust, he thought. Or perhaps his father's mild response was all part of the new politeness. There'd been a lot of it about lately. Too much in fact. He knew for example that it was no use getting interested in TV, which would be switched off the instant Tim walked in. 'The standard of etiquette in this house has gone through the roof,' he thought bitterly.

Tim knocked at seven on the dot. Mrs Hanley went to the door and ushered him into the room. He'd given her some flowers. He wasn't in uniform, but wore a grey suit.

'Good evening, sir,' he said. 'Hello, Tan.'

''Lo,' grunted Tan, staring intently at the screen.

'Good evening, Tim,' beamed Mr Hanley. 'Sit down, lad: she won't be a minute.'

'She will,' thought Tan. 'At least. And she's been an hour and a quarter already.' He wondered what would happen if the young officer were to see his sister without all that stuff on her face. He kept his gaze riveted to the screen in an extravagant display of interest, but it didn't do him any good. His mother walked over and switched it off.

'We don't need that thing on I'm sure!' she said, putting on her telephone voice. 'I must put these in water.' She hurried away with the flowers. Tim grinned at Tan. 'Start of the hols, isn't it?'

'Yes.'

'Looking forward to them, I'll bet!'

Anne walked in disguised as someone pretty and Tim's eyes went all dreamy. 'Oh, yes,' said Tan. 'I'm having a really fantastic time already.' It was a good line, he thought, but it was wasted on Tim, who had forgotten he was there.

6

Simon was waiting at the bottom of Cobden Street. He was gazing across at the Tangle and didn't see Tan approaching. At his friend's 'Hi!' he spun round as though shot.

'Oh; hi, Tan,' he said. 'I didn't hear you coming.'

Tan grinned. 'I know. Sorry I couldn't make it last night. Family trouble. You all right?'

Simon nodded. 'Sure. What d'you want to do?'

'I told your mum we'd be in the park, so I suppose we'd better go there for a bit. Where's Diane?'

'She's off buying shoes with Mum. She'll be around this aft.'

'Ah. Come on, then.'

They turned left and walked along the main road. There was some mist about, but the sun was behind it somewhere and it would probably warm up later on.

'How're the mice?' asked Tan casually. Simon looked uncomfortable. 'Dunno. I let 'em loose.'

Tan nodded. 'I thought so. Your mum said you went out with a box. Why didn't you let me have them, Simon?'

Simon shrugged again. 'They were wild, Tan. They're not the sort you keep.' Tan shot his friend a perplexed glance.

'You don't get wild white mice. Their parents must have been tame. They'd have been all right.'

Simon shook his head. 'I used to keep mice, Tan. These were different. Their feet were funny, and they spooked the guinea-pigs something shocking. You should have seen them cowering in corners, shivering. I had to get them out of there before they gave them heart-attacks or something.'

'I know,' Tan told him. 'It was the same with the gerbils, daft beggars. I decided to give it a day or two though. You could have kept 'em till I got there, surely?'

'You weren't coming,' said Simon. 'And anyway I love my guinea-pigs. Most of them were born in our shed, and I wasn't going to let 'em be frightened like that. Besides, I got to thinking about all the diseases wild mice carry. They're mucky things, y'know – they go in sewers and on dumps and that. You can't tell what they might pass on.'

'Well,' said Tan, 'I'm keeping mine, I can tell you that.'

Simon shrugged. 'Please yourself.' He began

walking towards the park and Tan fell in beside him. They turned in at the gateway and went up the path, kicking bits of gravel. The sun broke through the mist and struck sparks from the short wet grass.

7

The two boys played in the park till lunchtime. The watery sunshine had brought out a few pensioners and mothers pushing prams. The dew evaporated. Children came in twos and threes until all the swings were taken and there was a queue for the slide. Tan suggested moving to the Tangle but Simon shook his head and they stayed where they were. His friend had been unusually quiet and Tan guessed he was regretting having released his mice.

When they parted at the bottom of Cobden Street Tan said, 'Call for you at two?' Simon nodded. Tan watched him walk away with his hands in his pockets, then turned and began making his way home, reflecting ruefully on the fact that the holidays, which had got away to such a poor start last night, weren't getting much better.

There was nobody in at home. Anne was a clerk at Viners and his mother would be typing away at the airbase. Tan nearly always had lunch by himself in the holidays and he liked it. It was the only time he could guarantee there'd be no nagging or unexpected chores.

He groped in his pocket for his latchkey, let himself in and went through to the kitchen. His mother had left a tin of baked beans on the table with a note under it, as usual. He smiled. The note would say, 'Tan: there are fish fingers in the freezer. Leave things tidy and *turn off the gas*. Mum'. It might say beefburgers or sausage-rolls instead of fish fingers, but the rest would be the same. He wondered why she bothered.

He took the padlock keys from their hook over the fridge and went outside. He'd have a look in the shed before starting lunch.

In the fragrant dimness everything seemed normal. The gerbils were moving about and Tan could see that food had been eaten and water drunk. He knew that sick or badly frightened animals don't eat. He grinned, running a finger across the mesh of a cage. It was going to be all right.

He returned to the house and read the note. It was fish fingers. He put four under the grill, heated up the beans and buttered a slice of bread. When the food was ready he poured ketchup over it and ate hungrily, mopping up tomato-sauce with his bread and humming to himself. He wouldn't have been allowed to do either if his parents had been there.

42

When he'd eaten, Tan washed and wiped the things he'd used, put them away and checked the cooker. Then he went through to the living room, switched on the TV and flung himself into a chair. He watched the news and a kids' programme, then switched off and set off to call for Simon. Within half an hour he was to wish he'd stayed at home.

8

'D'you like them?' Diane had answered the door. She had her new shoes on. She stuck out a foot and wiggled it about. Tan looked at it gloomily. 'Yeah!' he mumbled. 'Great. Are you coming out?'

'Yes, but I'll have to take these off. Just a minute.' She disappeared into the house and he heard her yell for Simon. He'd be reading in the toilet. He always was. Said it was the only place he got a bit of peace.

A minute later brother and sister came tumbling out of the house and the three of them set off along the road. 'Let's go on the Tangle,' suggested Diane. Tan glanced at Simon to see if he'd object, but he didn't. Whatever had been bothering him that morning seemed to have receded, because he nodded and said, 'OK with you, Tan?' Tan said that it was.

There were some little kids messing about when they got there, but as soon as they spotted the older children the tots fled; scrambling madly up the slope and away through a gap in the fence. Tan grinned. 'They thought we were Deacon's lot.'

They walked down the slope and began picking their way along the bottom as usual. People dumped some strange things on the Tangle and the three friends never tired of looking for anything which might be new and interesting. Once, somebody had even left an old car there, and it had made a terrific gang headquarters till Deacon's dad had come one day and dismantled it, taking away the pieces in a van. Deacon's dad was a scrap metal dealer.

Today there was nothing spectacular. They walked up towards the tunnel. When they came to the mattress they'd found the mice in, Tan went and prodded about with his foot to see if the creatures had returned to their nest, but they hadn't.

'I know what we can do,' he said, kicking the mattress. 'We can set fire to this thing and pile other stuff on top – have a bonfire.'

'Oooh yes!' cried Diane. 'You got matches, Tan?'

'Sure.' He dug in his pocket. Simon looked dubious. 'What if the mice want to use it again?' he said. Tan shrugged.

'Tough,' he said. 'There's plenty of other places. Come on: get some paper and dry leaves and stuff.'

They hurried about, picking up sticks and

paper and last year's leaves. Tan made a pile of them up against the side of the mattress. As they worked, Simon seemed to lose his reluctance and soon he was shoving things into the pile with enthusiasm. Having bonfires was one of the most popular entertainments on the Tangle, and was one of the reasons why parents were uneasy about their children playing there.

When they had a large heap of dryish stuff, Tan struck a match and plunged it into the pile. A flame flickered among the bits and pieces, almost invisible because of the bright sunshine.

There was a crackling, hissing noise and a wisp of smoke. Tan straightened up. 'How about that!' he crowed. 'One match, after a winter like we've had.'

Once established the flames spread quickly. Soon, the mattress itself started to smoulder, sending up a column of thick, white smoke. The three friends dashed about, finding things to pile on top. Even wet items were all right now: the heat of the fire sizzled them dry in no time and the children piled them on, so that half the smoke that went billowing skywards was steam.

'Look at it!' yelled Diane. 'I bet they can see it the other side of town.'

'Deacon's trousers!' cried Tan. 'Go get Deacon's trousers, Simon.'

Simon ran off and came back dragging the horrible garment behind him. Tan seized it and draped it across the mattress, screwing up his eyes against the stinging smoke.

'Phew!' screeched Diane. 'What a stench.'

'What d'you expect?' laughed Simon. 'Deacon's pants and Deacon's mattress: they're not going to smell like perfume, are they?'

'No!' cried Tan. 'And those are his best trousers: think what his others must pong like!'

'Very funny,' snarled a deep voice behind them. The three friends whirled, and gasped with dismay. Deacon was standing at the foot of the slope, his fists on his hips. Two of his henchmen stood with him; one either side of their leader, and the rest of the gang were strung out across the slope, cutting off any possibility of escape.

'Now then, Hanley,' growled Deacon. 'What was that you were saying about my trousers, eh?' He advanced threateningly, his big fists at the ready.

Tan stepped back, looking wildly around. The far side of the Tangle was bordered by a two-metre wall. There were no boys on that slope, but he knew it afforded no chance. They'd never get over the wall, even if they reached it. He ran his tongue over dry lips and said, 'We weren't talking about you, Gary. There's this kid called Deacon in our school: John Deacon. We were talking about him.'

'No you weren't.' Deacon's eyes glinted

narrowly. 'There's no Deacons around here except us. You were on about me, and on my territory too. I'm gonna smash you, Hanley kid.' He moved forward and Tan retreated into the smoke.

'You leave us alone!' cried Diane. 'You're fourteen and we're only eleven and twelve. Pick on somebody your own size.'

'Fozz off!' growled Deacon. 'Craig; Shaun: grab her and the other one while I see to this creep.' Tan turned and ran for the tunnel but it was no use: Deacon's longer legs gave him the edge and he grabbed him in the open.

'No you don't, kid!' He twisted Tan's collar in his fist and yanked him round. Tan lashed out at his captor's brutal face but Deacon easily dodged the blow and his free hand closed like a vice on the smaller boy's wrist. 'Hit me, would you?' he sneered. 'Hit old Gary, eh? Well, we'll just have to teach you a lesson kid, won't we?' He lugged the helpless Tan back towards the fire.

Simon lay face-down in the grass, writhing. One boy sat on his back while another held his feet. Simon jerked his head from side to side, yelling, 'You leave my sister alone, you thick prannocks: leave her alone!' A few yards away, Diane lay on her back with a boy across her legs. Another lout held her wrists, while a hard-looking girl scooped up handfuls of dirt and smeared them on Diane's coat and jeans, hissing fiercely as she did so. 'Spoil your clothes,

48

eh? Dirty your nice clean clothes Miss posh-talk, eh?'

'Give over, Mandy!' Deacon, holding Tan like a broken doll, scowled at the girl. 'I never told you to do that. I said grab her, that's all. I decide what we do with 'em, right?'

The girl made no reply but wiped her hands in the grass and knelt, waiting. The boys had come down off the slope and were standing around, eleven of them, grinning in anticipation of some fun.

'Right!' said Deacon. 'This is what we do. We get some rope, tie these creeps up and dump 'em in the tunnel: right in. They'll be crying for their mammies before anyone comes to rescue 'em!'

Noises of approval greeted this plan, except from the boy sitting on Simon. He shook his head and said, 'No, Gary: you're too soft, man. There's a fire here, right? I reckon we ought to roast 'em, or smoke 'em at least.'

Deacon gazed at the boy for a moment in silence. 'You know what you are, don't you, Lacy?' The boy shook his shaggy head, grinning.

'You're one of them juvenile delinquents, mate. We'll all be coming to see you in Borstal if you don't watch it. Didn't your mummy ever tell you roasting people is wrong, lad?'

The boys laughed. He was a great joker, old Deacon. It was one of the things they liked about him.

'Right then,' he said. 'You spare lot start looking for something to tie 'em with while we get 'em in the tunnel.' The boys dispersed, trampling the long grass with their eyes on the ground. Deacon jerked his head at Diane and Simon. 'Get them on their feet and bring 'em over here.' He made for the tunnel, shoving Tan in front of him. The others were hauled erect and pushed along too.

'You can't leave us in there,' Tan protested. 'What if nobody comes? We could die and you'd be a murderer.'

Deacon laughed. 'No chance, kid. We're not gagging you. Someone'll come if you yell loud enough. Unless the ghost gets there first, I mean.'

The three children were hustled into the dank tunnel. Two boys came running, their hands full of worn electrical flex. 'Will this do, Gary?' one of them said. Deacon fingered the tangle of mouldering rubber and greenish wire. 'I suppose so,' he said. 'You do the girl, Colin. Hands behind, sit her down, tie her feet. Craig: the same with that one. I'll fix young Hanley here.'

There was nothing they could do. The rest of the gang watched from the mouth of the tunnel, silhouettes against the light; nudging one another and calling taunts into the darkness. The flex bit into the captives' wrists and the floor was filthy with ancient soot. When the last knot

50

was tied their captors carried them as far into the darkness as they dared go and laid them side by side on the ground. Deacon stood over them, smirking.

'Right then, you creeps!' he hissed. 'You were having a good laugh out there, so let's hear you laugh now.' He swung a kick at Tan's side. Tan gasped and curled up. 'Come on kid,' snarled the bully. 'Laugh.'

'Aren't you brave!' cried Simon. 'Kicking someone smaller when he's tied up. I bet you'd scream your head off if you met someone your own size.'

Deacon turned and looked down at him. 'You,' he growled, 'want to learn to keep it shut!' He prodded Simon with the toe of his shoe. 'I saw the look on your mug when I mentioned puttin' you in here. You went all white, kid. It's you who'll be screaming as soon as me and the lads clear off. Which we're doing right now,' he added, turning away. 'Come on Craig, Colin. Let's get out of here.' The three louts began making their way back to the entrance, sauntering off with their hands in their pockets. The children followed with their eyes. The silhouettes dwindled, joined up with the others and the gang moved away from the tunnel, their laughter fading.

'What we going to do?' whispered Diane. 'Shout?'

'Not yet.' Tan struggled against the flex which bound his wrists. 'That's what they want us to do. They'll be out there now, waiting to hear us yell so they can laugh. I might be able to get my hands free in a minute.' He writhed and grunted, rolling about in the dirt.

'I can't move mine,' said Diane. 'That big bully tied them really tight and it hurts.' She sat with her back against the wall, wiggling her feet in an attempt to loosen the wire round her ankles.

'I'm pretty hopeless too,' gasped Simon. 'There's a funny smell in here, isn't there?'

Tan paused in his struggle, sniffing. 'Yes,' he said. 'It is a bit peculiar. Reminds me of something but I can't think what.'

They fell to testing their bonds, and for a time nobody spoke. Presently, Tan broke the silence. 'My hands are a lot looser now,' he said. 'But I just can't loosen them enough to get free. What I need is somebody to have a go at the knots with his teeth, like they do in films sometimes. How about it, Simon?'

'Ugh!' Diane shivered. 'Bite that filthy flex? I wouldn't fancy it, Simon.'

Tan glared at her. 'Would you rather stay here then?' he demanded. 'Or start screaming so that rat Deacon can kill himself laughing? Come on, Simon: give it a try.'

Simon, who was farthest from the entrance, made no reply. Tan peered at him in the gloom. 'Hey Simon, are you listening?' The boy had his back to the others and seemed to be staring into the blackness. After a moment he said, 'There's something in there. I can see something white.' He spoke in a dry whisper and Tan knew he was scared. He hoped he wasn't going to start making a noise, proving Deacon right.

'What is it?' he asked. 'That old ghost again? Maybe he'll have a go at this wire if we ask him nicely.' He chuckled, hoping to joke Simon out of his fear. It didn't work.

'It's white, and it's not moving, and I can see it better now,' whispered the frightened boy. Tan screwed up his eyes, peering in the same direction. There was something. He could see it himself. Up against the wall of the tunnel, maybe fifteen metres away. Something white, which didn't move. He swallowed hard.

'I see it,' he said, struggling to keep his voice even. 'It's probably a sheet of old newspaper that's blown in. You can feel what a draught there is.' It was true. A steady stream of cold air flowed into the tunnel, carrying smoke from the fire outside. Where it went to he didn't know, because the other end was bricked up. Simon shook his head.

'It isn't paper,' he whispered. 'It's the wrong shape. I think it's a – I think it's ...' His voice trailed off in a broken sob, and he began to struggle violently; thrashing about, making little noises in his throat like a wounded animal. Tan rolled, trying to get to his friend, hoping to calm him by being close.

There was no need. With a hoarse cry, Simon wrenched his hands free of the flex and began tearing at the knots which secured his ankles. He cursed and gibbered as he worked, hunched up over his knees; tugging and tearing and picking until, with a shout of triumph, he whipped away the flex and leapt to his feet.

Tan, sensing that his friend might run, yelled sharply. 'Simon! Here: help us.'

Simon glanced wildly into the darkness then knelt swiftly, picking at Tan's bonds with fumbling fingers. Tan felt the wire give, wrenched it slack with a kick and slipped his feet through. 'Get Diane!' he gasped. 'I'm off to look.'

He rolled over and got up, his hands still tied. He was scared, but his hatred of Deacon was stronger than his fear of whatever lay there in the dark. He could hear Diane behind him, encouraging her brother. He'd go right up to the thing and prove it harmless, and then the three of them would walk out into the light as though nothing had happened.

As he neared the object it began to assume a definite shape. He slowed, his scalp prickling. He took one pace. Two. He screwed up his eyes, his mouth dropped open and a wave of ice-cold dread washed over him. There, in the angle of floor and wall, lay the remains of a man.

9

'What the heck d'we do?' They stood panting on the slope, gazing back towards the tunnel from which they had fled. The smoke was thinning out and there was no sign of the Deacon gang. Tan's knees wobbled and he felt sick. 'I don't know, Diane,' he said. 'Tell the police, I suppose.'

Simon rubbed his sore wrists. 'Of course we tell the police!' he cried. 'What d'you think we're going to do: put the skull in my collection and say nothing?'

Diane shivered. 'It might be that porter,' she murmured. 'The one who ...'

'Porter?' Simon shot her a scornful glance. 'That was years ago. You think they just left him there or something?'

'All right clever-clogs!' snapped Diane. 'You were scared, that's what's up with you. You were scared stiff and now you're trying to cover it up by being sarcastic.'

'No, I'm not!' the boy retorted. 'I was closest

to it, that's all. I was practically lying right next to it.'

'Were you heck!' sneered his sister. 'It was miles further in. I bet you'd have run off and left us if Tan hadn't shouted at you.'

'Give up, you two!' said Tan. 'We were all scared. Anybody would have been. We've got to tell the police and we'd better do it now. Do we go to the station, or should we phone?'

'Phone,' said Diane. 'It's quicker.'

'Right. There's a box outside the park. Anybody got a twenty?'

They delved in their pockets. Simon pulled out a twenty and they hurried towards the box.

There was a woman in the box. Tan felt like opening the door and interrupting her. 'Excuse me,' he'd say in a quiet, dramatic voice. 'But I have a vital call to make. A matter of life and death.' And it would be true: absolutely true. For the first time in his life he was having a real adventure, like kids do in books. Now that they were out of the tunnel he even felt quite brave and resourceful, and found himself looking forward to the stir which their revelation was bound to cause in the town.

They sat on the wall, drumming their heels in a fever of impatience while their eyes bored into the woman's back. A man came towards them. Tan was tempted to tell him what they'd found but he didn't. He knew that if he did, the matter would be taken out of their hands. The

56

man would call the police and it would be as though he'd discovered the body. In real life nobody takes much notice of kids but they would now, he told himself. They would now.

The woman finished her conversation and came out of the box. The children converged on it and Simon thrust his coin into Tan's hand. 'Here,' he said. 'You do it.'

Tan went into the box. Diane and Simon stood on the pavement, watching him through the glass. He flipped through the tatty directory till he found the number of the police station. For some reason his hands were trembling. He fumbled the coin into the slot and dialled carefully, biting his lip to quell his excitement. It occurred to him that there was something sick about getting a kick out of some poor man's death, but before he had time to pursue the thought somebody picked up the phone.

'Police. Can I help you?'

Tan swallowed and said, 'We've found a skeleton.' He'd meant his voice to sound firm but it came out as a sort of croak.

'I'm sorry madam,' said the policeman. 'I didn't quite catch that. Will you say it again, please?' Diane was leering through the glass. Tan stuck his tongue out at her and said, 'I'm a boy, and we've found a skeleton in Low Grange Tunnel.' It sounded daft.

'Sorry, lad. A skeleton, you say? What sort of skeleton?

'A man's,' said Tan. There was a brief silence, and then the policeman said, 'Are you having me on, lad?'

'N-no,' Tan stammered. 'No, I'm not. Deacon left us tied up in there and we saw it. It's got black clothes on.'

'Who's we?' the policeman asked.

'Us,' said Tan. 'Simon and Diane Playfair and me. I'm Tan Hanley.'

'And where are you calling from, Tan?'

'The phone box by the park on Grange Road.' He looked at the number behind its plastic disc. 'It's 35245.'

'All right, lad. Now listen. I want you and your friends to wait there by the phone box. Not inside, because somebody might want to use the phone, but don't go away. I'm sending a car, but I wouldn't be you if you're pulling my leg. Understand?'

'Yes,' said Tan. 'Thanks.' He replaced the receiver and left the box.

'What did they say?' asked Diane. Tan shrugged.

'Not a lot. Sounded bored and called me madam. Thought I was having 'em on. We've to wait here – they're sending a car.'

'Weee!' Diane clenched her hands and did a series of little jumps. 'Isn't it exciting? We'll be on TV and in the papers. We'll be famous!'

'Will we hummer.' Tan was looking at Simon, who stood with his shoulders hunched and his hands in his pockets, staring at the ground.

'What's up with you?' he demanded. 'You look like they're coming to take you away. You didn't do it, did you?' It was meant as a joke, but Simon didn't laugh. He didn't even smile. He shook his head and said quietly, 'No, Tan. Not me. But somebody did it, and I was just thinking it might easily have been one of us lying there.'

10

Tan shivered. 'Hmm. You're right, Simon. In fact I wouldn't be surprised if the murderer was in there that time we felt something creepy. Y'know – last year?'

Simon nodded. 'That's what I mean. I think we should keep away from that place from now on.'

'They're here!' cried Diane, who had been looking for the police car. They watched as it drew up nearby. Two uniformed figures sat inside. A man and a woman. They got out and came over.

'Which one of you is Tan Hanley?' asked the woman.

'I am,' Tan answered. She nodded and looked at the others.

'And you are Diane and Simon Playfair I take it?'

'Yes,' said Diane.

'Good.' The woman gave a brief tight smile and nodded towards her companion. 'This is

Police Constable Stables and I'm WPC Carter. You say you found a skeleton. A human skeleton, in Low Grange Tunnel?'

Tan nodded. 'Yes.'

'Well then, we'd like you to show us. Get in the car please.'

Constable Stables held open a rear door while the children got in. It was a new car with a clean, leathery smell inside. A few passers-by stared as they settled on the creaky seat. I bet they think we're being arrested, thought Tan.

They had only a few metres to travel. The woman drove, and Tan showed her the gap in the fence. The car stopped and they got out. 'Right.' WPC Carter looked through the gap. 'The tunnel's up that end, right?' The children nodded and she said, 'Come on, then.'

They began making their way down the slope. PC Stables locked the car, spoke into his clip-on radio and brought up the rear.

They turned right at the foot of the slope and walked up towards the tunnel. The old mattress, half-burned, was still smouldering. 'That yours?' said the woman, and Tan nodded again.

They reached the mouth of the tunnel. WPC Carter had a torch. She switched it on and played its beam into the darkness.

'How far in is it?'

'About twenty metres,' said Tan, pointing. 'This side. Shall I show you?'

'Yes, please.' She turned to the constable.

61

'Stay here with these two, Jim. I'll call if I need you.'

'Right-o.'

They went into the tunnel. It was easy by torchlight. When they were near the spot, Tan pointed. 'It's just there.' He felt sick and didn't really want to see the thing again, but he forced himself to look as the powerful beam picked it out.

WPC Carter uttered a little exclamation and Tan realized she had not really believed him till now. She squatted down and moved the light over the remains while Tan stood behind, unable to tear his eyes away.

The skeleton lay on its back. The jaws gaped and one arm lay across the chest as though flung there to ward off a blow. The man had been wearing a donkey jacket and dark corduroy trousers, and here and there some ragged shreds of a shirt were visible. The torchlight travelled down the body to reveal a pair of wellingtons with the tops turned over and the trousers tucked into them. Somebody had printed a name with a felt-tip pen on the canvas lining of one of the boots. The woman played the beam on this and Tan bent forward, screwing up his eyes. The canvas was dirty, the lettering smudged and blurred, but he was able to read the name 'I. BAIN'.

The policewoman straightened and said, 'Right, young man, let's get you out of here.' She laid an arm across Tan's shoulders and began propelling him gently towards the entrance, playing her torchbeam on the ground in front of their feet. Here we go, he thought. It's 'Thanks a lot, Kiddies: now run away and play' time. Aloud he said, 'Is it a murder, then?'

The woman shrugged. 'I don't know, Tan. He's been in here a long time by the look of him. It'll take an expert to say how he died. You'll read about it in the Gazette eventually.'

'Will they put us in the Gazette, d'you think?'

WPC Carter smiled in the darkness. 'Oh, I expect so, Tan. You did a good job, the three of you: acted exactly as you should. You might even get a letter from the Chief Constable.'

They came out of the tunnel. The woman spoke quietly to PC Stables, who took the torch and went to see for himself. Then she produced a notebook and pencil. 'Right,' she said. 'I'll just have a note of your addresses and then we'll let you go. Don't want to waste your holidays, do we?'

The children would gladly have wasted an hour or two waiting to see what would happen, but something in the woman's tone warned them not to argue. They'd done their duty. Now they were being packed off as usual. They gave their addresses. WPC Carter wrote them down and said, 'Thank you. You've been a real help to us today and we'll be in touch. Oh, and before I forget,' she looked at Tan, 'you said something on the phone about somebody tying you up and leaving you in the tunnel. What was that all about?'

The question startled Tan, who had practically forgotten about that part of the incident. He knew that if he wanted it, here was an opportunity to make trouble for Gary Deacon. He had only to tell this woman what had happened, and the bully would receive a visit from the police. It would not be his first.

But for some reason he could not have explained, Tan felt reluctant to tell on his tormentor. It wasn't that he was scared of what Deacon might do to him afterwards. He knew the lout would beat him up anyway, if he ever caught him on the Tangle again. It was something else: a feeling that he needed to find a better way of dealing with his foe. He shrugged and grinned. 'It wasn't anything,' he said. 'We were playing, that's all.'

The woman arched her brow. 'Are you sure, Tan?'

He nodded. 'Sure.'

'All right. Off you go then. Oh, and don't light fires, there's good kids – it is quite dangerous you know.'

They climbed the slope. When they were out of earshot Diane said, 'That was a bit of a drag, wasn't it? I mean, they didn't exactly get all excited, did they?'

'I expect they see dead bodies every day,' Tan

replied. 'Anyway, we're not going far. We can go along the fence a bit and watch through a hole. There'll be all sorts of people turning up in a bit.'

Simon, hands in pockets, aimed a vicious kick at a clump of coltsfoot. 'Why didn't you split on Deacon, you dummy?' he growled. 'You could have got him done.'

Tan shrugged. 'I dunno. I'd rather see to him myself, I suppose.'

'See to him?' Simon laughed mirthlessly. 'That'll be the day. You should have dropped him in it.'

Tan shook his head. 'No. You can laugh, Simon, but one of these days I'm going to fix Gary Deacon once and for all. You see if I don't. Where shall we watch from?'

'I'm not watching,' muttered Simon. 'I've had enough of this place for one day. See you.' He ducked through the gap and crossed the road without looking back. They watched him for a moment, then set out to find a vantage point.

11

Another car came. It was driven by a constable in uniform but the three men who got out were in ordinary clothes. They went through the gap and down the slope. 'Detectives!' hissed Tan. The constable stayed in the car but he couldn't see the children, who stood with their cheeks pressed against the fence, peering down through the slats at the patch of bare ground in front of the tunnel. There was a bus-shelter between them and the place where the gap was and, though they could watch for new arrivals through its glass panels, nobody was going to spot them unless they were really looking for them.

'Two of them might be detectives,' contradicted Diane, 'but one's a pathologist: the one with the bag. He's come to examine the body to try to determine the time of death and its cause.' Tan looked sideways at her.

'Thanks, Sherlock,' he growled. 'You're getting like your brother, you know.'

The three men walked along the Tangle and joined PC Stables and WPC Carter. They talked. Tan and Diane couldn't make out what they were saying. Now and then somebody would wave a hand towards the tunnel, and all five looked up a lot towards the road. PC Stables kept looking at his watch. 'They're waiting for somebody else to come,' whispered Diane.

Sure enough, almost immediately they heard the sound of a motor and a large blue van appeared, drawing up behind the two cars. Several men and women got out; some in uniform and others in civilian clothes. Some of them were carrying things: bags and boxes and a lot of poles and rolls of what looked like canvas.

'Looks like flippin' camping gear,' Tan remarked.

'It's a screen,' said Diane. Tan didn't argue. He knew with gloomy certainty she'd turn out to be right.

The men began carrying all the stuff down the slope. Two women got a reel of pink tape and some cones, and made a sort of flimsy fence on the pavement in front of the gap. 'To keep sightseers away,' whispered Diane. The activity had already attracted some onlookers who stood about on the other side of the road, talking and pointing.

When they'd finished the fence the two police-women stood side by side in front of it with their feet apart and their hands clasped behind them, gazing stonily across at the gawpers.

Down by the tunnel, things were happening. A lot of equipment was being carried inside and, while some of the men walked back and forth, others were planting poles in the ground and rigging up a screen. 'See?' said Diane.

Presently two men came up the slope carrying a reel, from which they paid out thick black cable. They laid it through the gap, under the fence of pink tape and into the back of the van. 'Lights,' said Diane. One of them stuck his head out and shouted something, and the inside of the tunnel was flooded with brilliant white light. 'For photographs,' said Diane. 'Shut your face,' said Tan.

The screen was progressing, and soon a section was erected between the children's vantage point and the scene they were watching.

They could still see heads moving about but a lot of the interest had gone, and after a moment Diane said, 'What time is it?' Tan glanced at his watch. 'Crikey!' he exclaimed. 'It's past four o'clock. Mum'll be home soon and I'm supposed to stick the vegetables on before she gets in. I'll have to go, Diane.'

The girl nodded. 'Me, too. Simon'll have told Mum and Dad about this and they'll think I'm getting in the way or something. It's a wonder Dad hasn't been down for me in the car.'

They turned reluctantly from the fence and were about to cross the road when they became

68

aware of some fresh activity near the police vehicles. A car pulled up and two people got out. One was a smartly-dressed young woman, the other a fattish man in a shabby mac, carrying what looked like a camera. They approached the two policewomen and an argument broke out. The children moved closer, using the bus shelter as cover.

'I bet they're reporters,' whispered Diane. 'From the Gazette.' Tan nodded.'They want to go through and the police won't let them.' They listened, peering through the grimy windows of the shelter. The photographer wasn't saying much, but the woman's voice was raised in strident protest.

'It's a disgrace!' she said. 'The people have a right to know what's going on and it's the job of newspapers to tell them.' One of the police-women said something in reply, but she spoke quietly and the children didn't catch her words. The reporter gestured angrily towards the gap.

'Who told you not to let us through?' she cried. 'Who's trying to gag the press? I demand to see your inspector or superintendent or whatever.'

Again, the policewoman's reply was too low for the children's ears. While his colleague argued, the photographer had sidled up to the fence and was attempting to aim his camera for a long-range shot of the activity round the mouth of the tunnel. A policeman stuck his head out of the back of the van and called something to him. The photographer turned, said something in reply and continued lining up his equipment. The policeman jumped down and strode towards him, whereupon he lowered his camera, lifted an open hand in a gesture of peace and moved away from the fence.

'I wonder why they're not letting them through?' said Tan. Diane shrugged. 'Dunno. P'raps it's all going to be hushed-up and we won't even know whose bones we found. P'raps he was someone important: someone famous or something.'

'Bain,' said Tan. 'I. Bain, his name was. It was in his welly. I've never heard of anybody famous called Bain, have you?'

'No,' Diane admitted. 'It's Scottish, isn't it?'

'I think so,' said Tan. 'Look.'

A second policeman had appeared and the press was in retreat. The photographer stowed his gear in the back seat while the woman made for the driver's door, walking backwards, arguing. A knot of onlookers still lingered on the far pavement, watching the fun.

The car doors slammed and the woman gunned the engine. The car backed up, pulled round the police vehicles and accelerated towards the two children. They waited at the kerb for it to pass.

It had barely done so when, with a squeal of brakes, it jerked to a stop. The woman got out and looked back at them across its shiny top. 'Does either of you two know the kids who found the body?'

Tan looked sideways at Diane. 'Do I tell her?'

'Why not?' said Diane. 'We might get famous yet.'

'Sure,' Tan called to the woman. 'We found it.'

The woman bent and said something to the photographer, who twisted round in his seat and unlocked a rear door. 'Get in,' said the woman as it swung open.

The children hesitated, unsure as to whether they ought to accept her invitation. For one thing, they'd been taught since they were tots that you don't get into cars with people you don't know. And then there was the fact that the police had seemed unwilling to tell this woman anything. If the police wouldn't tell her, was it all right for them to do so?

The woman glanced back along the road. 'Come on, kids,' she urged. 'Don't you want to be in the paper? Rod here takes a terrific picture!'

Diane looked at Tan. 'Well?' she said. 'We did want a bit of excitement out of it, didn't we?' Tan hesitated a moment longer, then grinned. 'Yes,' he said. 'We did, didn't we?' They ran to the car and scrambled in.

'Good for you!' The woman slid in behind the wheel, slammed her door and the car took off on screaming tyres.

They didn't go far. A quick dash, a couple of heart-stopping corners and the car came to a smooth halt in a little-used cul-de-sac. 'Now then,' the woman grinned. 'Let's talk. My name's Liz Gordon: what're yours?' They told her. 'Mind if we have this on?' She reached into the glove-compartment and held up a little tape-recorder. The children shook their heads, but she noticed Tan's troubled frown. 'What's the matter, Tan?' she asked. 'Unhappy about this, are you?'

Tan, smiling sheepishly, nodded. 'I don't know if we should be doing this,' he said. 'The police wouldn't talk to you, would they?' The woman smiled.

'No, Tan,' she said. 'They wouldn't. But you see, when it comes to murder, the police tend not to trust newspaper people. They think we might print something that will help the murderer. They don't give us credit for much intelligence.' She smiled again. 'Do you think I'd print anything which might help a murderer, Tan?'

Tan felt himself beginning to blush. He liked Liz Gordon. She had a nice smile. He looked down and shook his head.

'Right.' She switched on the recorder and asked how they came to discover the body. She asked what it looked like and if there had been anything near it – a weapon perhaps, or a note. Anything. Tan told her no. He told her about going back in with WPC Carter and seeing the name I. Bain in the wellington boot. 'There isn't much more I can tell you,' he said. 'We came out of the tunnel and she more or less told us to shove off. Simon went home, and Diane and I watched from the road.'

The reporter nodded. 'And what did you see, Tan?' The boy shrugged. 'Nothing much. Some plain-clothes men came.'

'And a pathologist,' put in Diane.

'Yes – a pathologist. They rigged up some lighting in the tunnel and then they put that screen up so we couldn't see. We were just leaving when you came.'

'I see.' Liz Gordon was silent for a moment. The spools of the little recorder whirred. 'And you didn't see anything that might suggest how this man met his death?' Tan shook his head. 'No.'

The reporter switched off the recorder. 'That's fine, Tan. I'm grateful to you both for talking to me. We'd better get you home now.'

She put the recorder back in the glove-compartment.

'What about the photo?' asked Diane.

'Photo?' The woman's eyebrows went up again. 'Ah, yes: I nearly forgot. Rod?'

'OK.' The photographer reached for his camera. 'Let's have you outside, kids.' They got out and Rod made them stand side by side with a wall behind them. 'Watch the birdie,' he said. Tan grinned and the man shook his head. 'No, lad: don't smile. You've just found a body, remember? We don't want it to look as though it's your hobby.'

He took four shots and they got back in the car. Tan looked at his watch. 'My mum'll go mad,' he said. Liz Gordon smiled. 'We'd better drop you off first, then.' She started the car and Tan directed her to his house. They drew up by the gate. To his surprise, the reporter got out with him. 'Come on, Tan,' she grinned. 'I'll have a word with your mum!'

His mum looked aghast when she heard about the skeleton, but Liz Gordon said it was her fault Tan was late and she said she understood. She even offered the reporter a cup of tea but the woman declined, explaining that Rod was waiting in the car and that anyway, she had to get Diane home. On the doorstep, she offered her hand to Tan. He took it, blushing furiously, and they shook. 'Thanks again, Tan,' she smiled. 'The picture'll be in tomorrow's paper, and if I can do you a favour sometime, be sure and call me: OK?'

He stood watching as she walked down the path. As the car pulled away Diane waved, but he didn't notice. He'd found somebody he liked even better.

1 2

'I don't know what's going on down by the old station,' Tan's father remarked, 'but there were police all over the place when Anne and I drove past just now.'

It was six o'clock and the family was eating. Tan, toying with his slice of flan, waited for his mother's inevitable response. It came.

'I fancy Tan can enlighten you, dear,' she said. 'He's had quite an adventure today, haven't you, Tan?'

Tan nodded gloomily. He didn't want to talk about it. Not to his father. He knew that as soon as his father heard about the body, he'd slap an out-of-bounds rule on the Tangle, probably for ever. He'd hoped his mother might not mention the matter, but deep down he'd known she would. She'd have brought it up, even if his father hadn't said anything about the police. They were looking at him now, expectantly. All three of them. He sighed.

'We found a body,' he said.

Mr Hanley laid down his fork. 'What did you say?'

'A body, in Low Grange Tunnel.'

'What sort of body, Tristan? What d'you mean?'

Tan lifted his glass and took a sip of water. Why was it, he wondered, that his father always sounded angry when he questioned him? He put down the glass. 'It was a man's body,' he said. 'A skeleton. I. Bain, he was called.'

Anne laughed; a sudden yelp. Her parents glanced at her sharply and she flushed, covering her mouth with her hand. 'Sorry,' she spluttered. 'It was the idea of a skeleton having a name.'

'Hmm.' Mr Hanley turned back to Tan. 'How did you come to find this body; who was with you?'

Tan told his father the whole story. When he had finished, Mr Hanley was silent for a while. Then he said, 'I've never liked the idea of your playing about in that place. It's not much better than a rubbish-tip, and that old tunnel is probably dangerous. Anyway, I want you to stay away from it from now on: is that understood?'

Not merely understood, thought Tan. Predicted. He nodded. 'Yes, Dad.' He hadn't promised: only confirmed that he understood.

He couldn't have said why, but he had the feeling that his involvement with the Tangle was not over yet. Not by a long chalk. He finished his meal in silence, excused himself, and went out to look at his mice.

1 3

'The Tangle's out of bounds,' said Diane, when Tan called for his friends the following morning. 'Old Simon here told Mum and Dad a really spooky tale about what happened yesterday, and they said we weren't to go there any more. Drag, isn't it?'

Tan, hands in pockets, nodded. 'Same with my lot,' he growled. 'I didn't promise, though. I'm off to see if the cops are still there, anyway. You coming?'

'No, we're not!' said Simon. 'We did promise. And anyway, I don't feel like going. I don't like the Tangle any more: there's something funny about it.'

'Something funny about you!' retorted his sister. She gazed wistfully at Tan. 'We did promise, though. D'you mind if we don't come? We could meet you in the park after.'

Tan shrugged. 'Suit yourselves. It'd be a bit boring though, wouldn't it, if the Famous Five spent all their time playing on the swings or something, because they'd promised? Wouldn't make a very gripping series on TV, would it?' He turned away, making for the gate. Diane called after him.

'Don't be like that, Tan. The Famous Five always have parents in America or something. They don't break promises, because they're not asked to make them in the first place. They're just stories.'

Tan turned in the gateway. 'You'll have parents in Birmingham tomorrow,' he mocked. 'Only difference is, you let 'em drag you along too. See you!'

He was being unfair and he knew it. If his own parents had been going away, he'd have had no choice but to go with them. He was angry because the Playfairs were off to Birmingham tomorrow and he'd be left on his own. He didn't enjoy being alone and he was taking it out on his friends.

He walked down Cobden Street and stood at the bottom, looking across Grange Road towards the dilapidated fence. The barrier of pink tape was still there, and a policeman was standing near it. A van was parked at the kerb. It was the same one that had been there yesterday, because he could see the thick black cable snaking away through the gap. He crossed the road and approached the policeman.

'Morning,' he said. The constable eyed him suspiciously.

'Morning, sonny. Something you're wanting, is there?'

Tan shook his head. 'No. Not really. I just wondered how things were going, that's all.'

'None of your business son, is it?'

'Yes it is,' Tan told him. 'I found the body.'

'Ah!' The man nodded. 'Well: we're taking care of it, son, don't you worry. You can safely leave it in our hands, I reckon. Better not be found loitering around here lad: better be on your way in fact. All right?'

Tan nodded, trying to see through the gap. The policeman shifted to block his view.

'Do they know what killed him yet?' he asked. The policeman frowned. 'Look, son,' he said. 'I've asked you to move on and you're still here. Do you want me to get nasty, lad? Is that what you want?' He advanced a pace, reaching for his pocket. Tan backed off.

'No!' he said quickly. 'I'm going. I just thought I'd ask, that's all. Only we found a dead cat, too. P'raps there's a mass-murderer about.'

'Gercha!' The constable raised his fist and took a quick stride in Tan's direction. Tan turned and fled.

1 4

The park was full of kids. Diane and Simon were on the swings. There was no empty swing, so Tan sat down on a bench. They saw him, but they didn't come over straight away and he knew they were paying him back for what he'd said. He sat with his hands in his pockets, whistling to show he didn't care and kicking bits of gravel. When they thought they'd kept him waiting long enough, his friends left their swings and came and sat with him.

'Did you see anything?' asked Diane. Tan shrugged.

'Police. They're still there. I talked to one, but he wouldn't tell me anything. Wouldn't let me look through the gap, either. I reckon there's something up: something special.'

'Rubbish!' Simon hacked at the pathway with the toe of his sandal. 'It's always like that when somebody's found dead. The police have to find out how he died, and if they let all the gawpers in, vital clues might be destroyed. There's nothing unusual about it.'

'Thank you, Captain Kojak,' said Diane sarcastically. She turned to Tan. 'What time does the Gazette come out?'

'About two o'clock I think,' he said. 'We get ours delivered at teatime.'

'So do we,' the girl replied. 'But I'm not waiting for that. I vote we go along to Roper's at two and buy one ourselves. I can't wait to see that picture.'

'They probably haven't used it,' said Simon. 'They take loads of pictures, y'know: hundreds. And they only use a few.'

'Oh, shut up, misery!' Diane retorted. 'You're only jealous because you're not in it. Of course they'll use it: it's the only one they've got and it's ages since there's been a murder in Market Fulford.'

'Might not be a murder, Diane,' cautioned Tan. 'That guy Bain might have crawled into the tunnel and just died. He might have been a drunk or something.'

'Just think,' Diane looked at the children playing all round them, 'all these kids, and we're the only ones who know about the body.' Tan nodded, grinning.

'They'll know tomorrow. We'll probably be mobbed when we come in here!'

'We won't be here,' Simon reminded them. 'We're off to Birmingham, remember?'

'Not till afternoon,' protested Diane. 'We could come for a while.' Simon shook his head.

'You must be joking. You know what it's like. In the bath, best clothes on, Mum panicking about all over the place, Dad fussing with the car. It's like getting ready for a trans-polar expedition.'

'Hmm,' said Diane, crestfallen. 'Yes, I know. You'll have all the glory to yourself, Tan.'

'I'd still rather you weren't going,' he replied. 'Don't forget to leave the key to the guinea-pig hut, or they'll all have starved when you get back.'

They messed about on the slide for a while, then went home for lunch. It was Good Friday, so nobody was working and Tan's mother had his meal ready. It was fish.

'Where've you been this morning, Tan?' his father asked as the family sat round the table.

'In the park,' said Tan. 'Simon and Diane were there.'

'You sure you haven't been hanging about that dump you call the Tangle?'

'No, Dad. You can ask Simon and Diane.' He knew his father would do no such thing, and he felt a bit guilty about lying. Still, he told himself, it wasn't a lie really: he hadn't hung about on the Tangle. He hadn't actually been on it at all, in fact.

'I could have done with a bit of help with the

car,' his father continued. He'd been cleaning it. Tan nodded.

'Yes. Sorry, Dad: I'd promised to meet the others, you see.'

'And this afternoon?' put in his mother. 'Have you promised to meet anybody this afternoon?'

'Yes, Mum.' He groaned inwardly, wishing he knew how to please his family. He was fed-up with being got at all the time. Unexpectedly, the opportunity presented itself.

'Anne and I are going to church this evening,' his mother told him. She didn't ask if he'd be joining them. He was off church at the moment, and they didn't discuss it much. He decided it was time to make a conciliatory gesture.

'Can I come with you?' he asked. The family looked at him in astonishment. 'Yes, of course you can,' said his mother. Anne glared at her brother over a forkful of peas. 'I hope you mean to behave,' she said, grimly. 'Tim will be with us.'

'Must be my lucky day,' said Tan. Perhaps, if he went along and conducted himself like a model member of the congregation, he'd be able to confess afterwards that he had mice in the shed, without causing too much of a hoo-ha. That was the idea, anyway.

At two, he met the Playfairs at the bottom of Cobden Street and they went along to the local newsagent for a copy of the Gazette. Mrs Roper smiled at them. 'I know what you want that for,' she said. 'It's on page three.'

The page one headline read, 'Man Found Dead In Tunnel'. The accompanying picture was a plan of the Tangle, with a white cross showing the position of the body in the tunnel. Tan opened the paper. There they were, Diane and himself, standing serious-faced in front of a brick wall. Mrs Roper came round the end of the counter and peered at the picture.

'Cost five pounds to talk to you now, I suppose,' she said. 'Ten,' said Tan. 'And five more for the autographs.' They left the shop and took the paper into the park, where they sat down on a bench in a quiet corner. Tan read the story aloud. There wasn't a lot to it, really. Children playing on the site of the former Market Fulford railway station had stumbled on the remains of a man in Low Grange Tunnel. Police were investigating, but a spokesman had declined to make any statement for the moment.

Little was known about the man, except that he had been wearing a donkey jacket, corduroy trousers and wellingtons. One of the wellingtons had the name 'I. Bain' written inside it. It was believed that Mr Bain was not a local man, and that his body had been in the tunnel for some time.

'They didn't get any of that from the police,' said Diane. 'It all came from us. They should pay us ten-thousand pounds for our exclusive story.'

'Lock you up more likely,' growled Simon.

'Newspapermen don't lock people up,' the girl retorted.

'The police, stupid. For divulging classified information.'

'Classified my foot.' Tan folded the paper and stood up. 'What shall we do now?'

'We could go into the town-centre and walk about,' said Simon sarcastically. 'See if people recognize you.'

'Jealousy will get you nowhere,' said Diane.

'Oh, come on you two,' said Tan. 'It's our last afternoon. Let's not waste it in fratching.'

They went back to the swings for a while, then sat in the park's wooden café drinking coke. The rolled Gazette protruded from Tan's pocket. The woman in the café had a copy too, and she kept looking across at them. After a while Tan said, 'Come on,' and they got up and left. It was nearly four o'clock. They were going to have to split up soon and there didn't seem to be much point in prolonging the agony. They turned homeward.

At the bottom of Cobden Street, Simon gave Tan the key to the shed. 'Here,' he said. 'Look after the beasts for me, and don't take any of those ghastly mice in there.' Tan grinned.

'Have a nice time in Birmingham.'

Diane pulled a face. 'Fat chance. See you, Tan.'

He stood for a moment, twirling the key on its bit of dirty string, then he turned and made for home.

15

The service was over and Tan was glad. The sermon had had a lot in it about cold, dark tombs and the business of dying, and Tan hadn't been able to keep himself from thinking about the skeleton in Low Grange Tunnel. All the time the vicar was speaking he had felt that people were looking at him. They probably weren't, but he had felt bad anyway. He'd sat with his arms folded and his head down, willing the sermon to end. He'd even wondered briefly whether the vicar had chosen his theme with Tan in mind, which he knew was rubbish. Still, he was glad when it was over.

Anne had gone off somewhere straight afterwards with Tim in Tim's car, leaving Tan and his mother to enjoy the short walk home. Tan walked with his hands in his pockets, breathing deeply the cool air of the evening. He'd hated every minute in church but he'd behaved perfectly. It was time to mention the mice.

'Mum?'

'What is it, Tan?'

'Mum: me and Simon found these baby mice that had been abandoned by their mother. They'd have starved to death, so we took them.' His mother looked at him, suspicion in her eyes.

'Took them? Where did you take them, Tan?'

'There were five,' said Tan. 'He took three and I took two. Mine are in the spare cage in the shed.'

'Oh, Tan!' his mother cried. 'Not mice. Not in our shed. It's too near the house, love. They attract wild ones, you know.'

'Only if you leave their food lying about,' said Tan. 'I've been doing the cage out every night and there's no smell at all. And they are only babies, Mum. If I chuck 'em out now they'll just die. Let me keep them till they can fend for themselves Mum; please!'

His mother pursed her lips and frowned. They turned a corner, coming in sight of the house. Tan eyed her anxiously. She saw his expression and smiled. 'All right, Tan, if it's that important to you. But you must promise me you'll keep them very clean, and even then I don't know what your dad'll say. You know what he's like about mice.'

Tan grinned, happy now that his secret was out. 'Thanks, Mum! You can make it all right with Dad, I know you can.'

They turned in at the gateway. His mother paused and looked at him gravely. 'There's one more condition, Tan,' she said.

'What's that, Mum?'

'Those two mice might be male and female. You must make another cage and separate them. Mice breed very quickly and we don't want to end up with a shedful. Do it tomorrow, Tan, before they get any older.'

'OK,' said Tan. 'I promise.'

His mother smiled at him and they went into the house. In the dark shed, the creatures Tan called mice clung together in a corner of their cage. Tomorrow they would be separated, but tomorrow would be too late.

16

Tan stuck his head round the kitchen door. 'I've done the cage, Mum!' He'd been up and about since seven, sawing lengths of wood from an old palette his father had brought from the cannery and knocking them together to make a small cage. It was a rough and ready thing, with a sheet of perforated zinc where the bars should have been. You couldn't see into the cage through the zinc, but he had nothing to make bars with so it would have to do.

'Well done, love!' His mother was still upstairs. 'Don't go away, will you? Breakfast won't be long.' She'd spoken to her husband about the mice and he had agreed, somewhat grudgingly, to Tan's keeping them till they were grown.

Tan went back to the shed and busied himself cleaning out the gerbils. He took his time and did a thorough job, because he knew that without Simon and Diane it was going to seem a long day. He fed the animals, changed their water and took a peep at the mouse he'd moved.

It seemed to have settled in all right. He swept the floor, put away his tools and went in to breakfast.

It was a long day. He wiped the breakfast things for his mother and went with her to the supermarket to carry the bags because his father had the car in bits. After lunch he helped with the car, reflecting gloomily that Anne would probably have roped him in for some boring task too, if she hadn't gone out for the day with the fantastic Tim. He was looking forward to going down to Simon's place and seeing to the guinea-pigs, but he knew there was no point in going before evening. Simon would certainly have fed and watered them before the family left for Birmingham, and he'd have locked up the shed with his second key. He told himself he was lucky still to have his mice, and that he ought to be thankful he wasn't being dragged off to Birmingham to stay with some ancient relative, and so teatime rolled round eventually and that was all right, except that Anne brought Tim home to share the meal with them.

As soon as the meal was over, Tan excused himself and set off for the Playfair house. The sun wouldn't set for over an hour yet, and it was a warm evening. He went round the long way, so that he could see if the police were still guarding the Tangle. They were.

At Simon's place he let himself into the shed

and spent half an hour cleaning out the guinea-pigs' quarters. It was funny how big guinea-pigs seemed when you were used to dealing with gerbils. He played with them for a while on the bench the cages stood on; calling them by their names and making them clamber over his hands. Maggie and Tarzan, Dick and Jane. He wondered if there were any little guinea-pigs on the way.

It was after seven when he coaxed the animals back into their cages and secured them. He took a last look round the twilit shed, let himself out and locked the door. The sun had gone down behind the houses, leaving an orange glow in the western sky. He was in no great hurry to get home, so he set off to go the long way round again. He was turning out of Grange Road into Cobden Street when a car pulled up beside him and Liz Gordon got out.

'Hello, Tan,' she said. 'I was just on my way to your house. Can you spare a minute?'

Tan felt himself blushing. He wanted to tell her he'd spare fifteen years if she asked him but he didn't. Instead he gawped at her and stammered 'Y – yes, I can.'

'Good.' She gave him a quick smile. 'Come and sit in the car, then. I want to ask you something.'

They got into the car. Tan looked sidelong at the woman, who was gazing blankly through the windscreen. 'What did you want to ask me?' he murmured.

'What?' She started, as though he'd woken her. 'Oh, yes. It was about the body, Tan. You don't mind talking about it, do you: only I don't want to upset you or anything?'

He shook his head. 'It doesn't upset me, Miss Gordon.' She smiled again, that same brief smile. 'Call me Liz. You said the body was a skeleton, Tan. What was it like exactly?'

Tan looked at her. 'Well,' he said. 'It was bones: just bones with clothes on them.'

'Are you sure about that, Tan?' She was gazing intently into his face. He nodded. 'Sure. It was a skeleton, like in a horror movie. Why d'you ask that?' He couldn't bring himself to call her Liz.

'Because, Tan,' she said slowly, 'four days ago, your Mr Bain was very much alive.'

For a moment Tan couldn't see what the woman was driving at. He gazed at her, waiting for her to continue. Then it hit him.

'Four days?' he gasped. 'People don't turn into skeletons in four days, do they?'

Liz Gordon shook her head. 'No, Tan, they don't. Not under ordinary circumstances. It takes weeks out in the open. Months sometimes. In that tunnel it should have taken longer. Years perhaps. There's something funny about it and I think that's why the police aren't saying anything.'

Tan frowned. 'How d'you know the man was alive four days ago?'

'Somebody phoned the office, Tan. A woman. She'd seen the story in the Gazette. She knew Bain. He'd lodged at her house all winter. He was a labourer, working on the new bypass. Four days ago he gave her the rent he owed and said he was leaving. He didn't say why, or where he was going. He crammed his belongings into an old holdall and left. That was Tuesday. You found his bones on Thursday. Two days. It doesn't make sense.'

'Why did the woman phone you?' Tan asked. 'Why not the police?'

The reporter shrugged. 'The police called on her. Yesterday. Told her Bain was dead, and that they'd traced him to her house through the firm he'd been working for. The firm's name was on the back of his donkey jacket. They asked her some questions, looked in Bain's room and left. When she read the bit in the Gazette about the body's having been in the tunnel for some time, she thought we'd made a mistake and phoned to tell us.'

'Wow!' Tan chewed his lip. 'So we know something nobody else knows: something we're not supposed to know. What did you say to the woman?'

Liz Gordon smiled. 'I thanked her for calling and said yes: it seemed we had made a mistake. Then I went to my editor. Told him what the woman had said and also what you'd told me about the body being a skeleton. I said I thought

94

there was a big cover-up going on and that we ought to splash it in Monday's paper.'

'And what did he say?'

'He said no.' There was disappointment in the woman's voice; a touch of bitterness. Tan glanced at her. It was almost dark now and he couldn't see her expression. He was groping for something to say when she continued.

'Y'see, Tan,' she said. 'I happen to believe newspapers should tell people the truth. That's what newspapers are supposed to be for. Things do get covered up: important things, and I think newspapers have a duty to uncover them if they can. Sometimes, a paper does uncover something, and it nearly always does a lot of good. But many a time, a newspaper will get to know something important and then not print it. What my editor will do is, he'll talk to the police: ask them if he can use the story. And of course they'll say no. They can't stop him, but they'll say it's not in the public interest or something, and he won't print it.'

'What's public interest?' asked Tan. 'D'you mean people wouldn't be interested in it?'

'No, Tan.' She smiled in the darkness. 'It doesn't mean that. It means – well, it means people might worry about it if they knew.'

He shrugged. 'Perhaps they might.'

'Yes,' she said. 'Perhaps. Anyway, I just thought I'd check the skeleton bit with you. Where are you going now?'

95

He told her he was on his way home, and she drove him there. The lamps made orange flashes in the car as they went under them. She stopped by the gate.

'Here we are, then. Thanks for talking to me, Tan.' She reached across him, opened the door and said, 'What's Tan short for?'

'Tristan,' he replied. 'Why?'

The woman shrugged. 'I just wondered. Nice name.' He undid the seat-belt and got out. 'Thanks for the lift, Liz. I'll see you.'

Halfway up the path he turned to watch her tail-light dwindle. Nice name. He wished he was called Jeff Sabre, the ace press photographer.

17

The sun felt warm on the back of Tan's neck as he stood at the top of the banking, looking down into the Tangle.

It was Friday. The week had passed slowly for him. He was looking forward to Simon and Diane's return tomorrow. There'd been nothing new in the paper about the mysterious death of Mr Bain. The police had withdrawn from the Tangle on Thursday and he was here, to see what they'd left behind.

There was nothing much so far. Just a patch of mud by the gap where they'd worn the grass away and a trampled path to the bottom. He went down, and made his way towards the tunnel. A part of him knew he ought not to be here, especially alone, but with the sun shining and birds twittering it was hard to imagine there could be any danger.

The bare ground in front of the tunnel was scarred and pitted with the marks of police activity. There were a couple of broken stakes, and

97

holes where others had been hammered in to support the screen. The charred remains of the mattress had been dragged to one side and lay at the foot of the banking, half-hidden by grass.

He didn't go into the tunnel. He wasn't exactly frightened, but he didn't fancy it. For one thing, Deacon might sneak up on him while he was in there. He glanced about quickly but he was alone. Everybody's parents had placed a fresh ban on the Tangle, and he knew that until it wore off a bit he was likely to have the place to himself. Except for Deacon. Nothing was ever out of bounds to him.

Tan mooched about, playing with the broken stakes. He fitted a piece into one of the holes, and threw another like a spear at what was left of the mattress. He was retrieving it when a movement caught his eye, and he saw a white mouse near his foot. Its whiskers quivered and it seemed to be looking up at him.

Anxious not to frighten the creature he remained in a stooped attitude, holding the stake.

'Hi!' he whispered. 'You must be Mummy mouse. Or Daddy. Did you get your babies back?' He half expected the little animal to dart away but it didn't. It squatted inches from his shoe, watching him.

'If you're worried about the other two,' he continued, 'you needn't be. I'm looking after them really well. They have all the food they need and fresh water and warm bedding. They're better off than they'd be here, I can tell you.' His back was beginning to ache. As soon as he moved the mouse would be off, but he couldn't stand like this much longer. 'Off you go then,' he whispered. 'And stop fretting.' He straightened up.

The mouse didn't move. Tan grinned. 'You're a brave one, aren't you?' he said. 'Either that or stupid. If I were a cat you'd be a goner by now, wouldn't you? Go on!' He stamped his foot. The mouse stayed where it was.

'Go on – scram!' He extended his foot towards the creature and was about to give it a gentle nudge when he noticed a second mouse watching him from beneath a clump of dock. No sooner had he spotted this than he saw another, and then a fourth. He felt a stab of unease and looked quickly about him. There were mice everywhere, watching through little pink eyes.

Suddenly he was scared. He didn't know why. They were only mice. Mice that appeared out of nowhere with their hard little eyes and twitching snouts. He began backing away. He moved slowly, gripping the stake like a club. The mice followed with their eyes but didn't stir. As soon as he felt flat ground under his shoes he spun round, flung the stake from him and ran.

He ran along the track and diagonally up the slope to the gap in the fence. There he paused, panting, and looked back. He scanned the undergrowth but as far as he could tell he had not been followed. The idea of being chased by mice suddenly struck him as absurd. A line from a half-remembered nursery rhyme repeated itself in his head as if to mock him. They all ran after the farmer's wife. They all ran after the farmer's wife.

He breathed out slowly, shaking his head. Thank God nobody had seen him. He got a brief mental picture of Liz Gordon watching his ignominious flight from the top of the slope. He groaned, feeling himself redden. What an idiot. What a prannock. Thank God.

He went through the gap, crossed the road and turned into the park. It was full of kids, sliding and swinging and running about on the grass. Tan sat down on a bench and looked at his watch. It was eleven o'clock. His cheeks began to cool. This time tomorrow Simon and Diane would be nearly home. Roll on. He wondered what they'd say when he told them what he'd just seen.

18

Next morning Tan woke early. He'd slept badly after a nightmare in which his wardrobe door had swung open releasing an avalanche of white mice.

He got up at six. The Hanleys slept late at weekends and it was no fun tiptoeing about the house, so he went out to the shed.

One of the mice was looking suspiciously plump. He picked it up and ran his fingertips along its bulging flank. There were a number of soft, moving lumps beneath the skin. Tan groaned.

'She'll go mad,' he muttered, referring to his mother. 'She'll make me take the whole lot back to the Tangle straight away.' He gazed at the mouse in his palm.

'What am I going to do with you?' he whispered. 'Why'd you have to go and get pregnant, just when you've found a smashing place to live?' He lowered his hand to the cage door and tipped it. The mouse began sliding off and then he felt a prick as one of the creature's claws caught in his skin. He winced, took the mouse in his other hand and worked gently to free the claw. It was a curved, fish-hook of a claw and very sharp. He had to pinch the tiny leg between thumb and forefinger and wiggle the thing loose, trying all the time not to hurt the mouse. When it was done, he popped the animal into its cage and examined his palm. There were two minute punctures and a bead of blood:

'Hmmm.' He pulled a tissue from his pocket and dabbed at the wound. 'I suppose that's what Simon meant when he said their feet were funny. I'll have to be careful about handling 'em in future.'

He left the shed and set off for the Playfairs' house.

He decided to go the long way round. It was a bit early to be prowling around somebody else's property and if he strolled to the bottom of Cobden Street and along Grange Road it would pass a bit of time.

He turned into Grange Road. A milk-float was parked on the other side, near the fence which separated the road from the Tangle. A milkman was standing by the fence, looking over. When he heard Tan's footfalls he turned.

'Hey, lad!' he called in a stage-whisper. 'Come over here, quick!'

Tan pointed a finger at his own chest.

'Me?' The milkman nodded impatiently. 'Yes, you. Hurry up, will you?'

Tan glanced up and down the road. It was empty. He crossed.

The milkman's hands gripped the top of the fence. Tan stood on tiptoe to see over. 'What's up?' he asked.

'Ghost,' hissed the milkman. 'Down there – see?' He stabbed the air with his finger. Tan looked where he pointed. There was a clump of little birches and what looked like a tyre in the grass. He shook his head. 'I don't see anything.'

'Keep watching,' growled the milkman. 'Behind the bushes.'

Tan strained his eyes. A breeze fluttered the birch leaves, which glinted in the early light. After a while he shook his head again. 'No. I can't see anything.' His feet hurt from standing on tiptoe. He gave up and turned away.

The milkman fixed him with a baleful stare, his hands still gripping the fence. 'It was there,' he insisted. 'It crossed the road right in front of the float. White, it was – about this high.' He levelled a palm two metres above the pavement. 'It walked clean through the fence. I jammed all-on and jumped out, and it was going down the slope there. It went behind the bushes and it hasn't come out 'cause I've been watching ever since.'

Tan looked along the fence. 'Where did it go

through?' The milkman relinquished his grip and pointed. 'There. About ten metres this side of the bus shelter.'

'There's a gap,' Tan told him. 'It probably went through the gap, whatever it was.'

'No.' The man shook his head. 'It didn't go through any gap. It went through the fence as if it wasn't there and you couldn't hear it either. If it had been anything but a ghost you'd have heard it in the grass but you couldn't. It sort of floated.'

Tan looked at the ground. The man was obviously agitated. Perhaps he was mad: some sort of crank.

'Well.' Tan shrugged and grinned. 'I'm sorry I missed it. P'raps you'll see it again tomorrow.'

The milkman looked over the fence with a wistful expression. 'Doubt it,' he growled. 'I've never seen it before and I'm here every morning. If you'd been half a minute sooner you'd have been a witness.' He sounded resentful.

A thought crossed Tan's mind. 'It wasn't mice you saw was it – hundreds of mice?' The man gave him a contemptuous look.

'Mice?' he sneered. 'What the heck're you talking about? I told you – it was this size.'

Tan nodded. 'Sorry,' he said. 'I've got to go now. Are you going to tell anybody: the papers or anything?'

'Naw.' The man shook his head. 'No point. Not without a witness. They'd think I was daft or drunk or something but I know what I saw, and it was a ghost.'

Tan nodded. 'That railwayman probably. Lots of people have seen him. 'Bye.'

The milkman replied with a curt nod. Tan crossed the road and went on. When he looked back, the man was still gazing over the fence. He turned up Fairfield Street. It was still only twenty to seven when he got to the house but there was nothing he could do about that. He cleaned out the cages, fed the guinea-pigs and did a general tidy-up of the shed. When he'd finished, he hung about a bit in the hope that his friends might arrive early. They didn't. He left a note for them and went home.

He didn't tell anybody about his encounter with the milkman. He trailed round the supermarket with his parents and spent the afternoon helping his dad with the car. It was half-past six when Simon knocked on the door.

19

'Hello, Mrs Hanley.'

'Hello, Simon. Come on in: Tan's just finishing the dishes. Have you had a good time in Birmingham?'

Simon pulled a face, wiping his feet on the mat. 'Not bad, thanks. There's not a lot to do at my gran's, but we did get about a bit while we were there. Ironbridge and Cannock Chase and this hill called the Wrekin. It's got an army firing-range on it.'

'Lovely. Sit down, Simon. I'll send Tan in.' She went through to the kitchen where Tan was wiping cutlery. 'Simon's here, Tan.'

Tan nodded. 'I know. I'm just finishing these.'

'I'll do that. You go through and talk to Simon. He's been to some interesting places.'

Tan went along to the living room. 'Hi, Simon. Nice time?'

Simon shrugged. 'OK. Thanks for looking after the animals. They seem fine.'

'No problem. Hey: one of the mice is going to have some babies.'

'Really? Can we look?'

'Sure. Come on.'

They went out to the shed. Tan opened the cage and lifted out the female mouse. He turned her in his hand so that Simon could see her slightly bulging sides. 'She is, isn't she?' Simon nodded. 'Looks like it. Have you told your mum you've got mice in here?'

'Yes. It was Mum who made me build this cage and separate the mice, only it was too late. I haven't told her about this yet.'

'Hmm.' Simon reached out, took the mouse from his friend and peered at it through his round glasses. 'It's funny,' he said. 'I'd have said they were a bit young yet for breeding. I reckoned they were about three weeks old when we found them.' He handed the creature back to Tan. 'I'd take them back to the Tangle and let them go if I were you. You could end up being inundated with them.'

Tan shook his head. 'No way. Not till I see what the babies are like. I've seen newborn gerbils, but not mice.'

'They're practically the same,' Simon told him.

'I still want to see them,' insisted Tan. He returned the mouse to its cage and they played with the gerbils for a while. It was dusk. They put the animals away and sat on the bench. Tan told Simon about the mice he'd seen, without mentioning his hurried retreat. He told him about the milkman too, and Liz Gordon. When he revealed that the unfortunate Bain had been reduced to bones in two days the other boy shivered and got down from the bench. 'Come on,' he said. 'Let's go outside.'

They stood in the twilit garden. 'I know you think I'm daft,' said Simon. 'But I wish you'd get rid of those mice. I don't know what it is but they give me the creeps. And if the ones on the Tangle breed as fast as these of yours, I'm not surprised there's hundreds of them. I've got to go now.'

Tan walked his friend to the gate. They said good night and he stood watching till the small figure merged with the shadows.

20

The new school term began on Wednesday. Wednesday's Gazette had a piece in it about Bain. Anne read it out at teatime when Mr Hanley had left the room and her mother was clearing the table.

'It says he came from Glasgow,' she said. 'Listen.' Tan leaned forward. 'Relatives of the dead man in Glasgow have said that in recent years Mr Bain had moved around the country, doing labouring work in the building industry. He often took lodgings close to his work, but in fine weather was in the habit of sleeping rough to economize on rent. Police now believe he may have been using Low Grange Tunnel for this purpose at the time of his death. A spokesman declined to comment on the cause of death but repeated that it was being treated as suspicious.'

"Course it's suspicious,' growled Tan. 'It's

109

more suspicious than they're letting on.'

His mother leaned across him and took his plate. 'How d'you mean, Tan?' Tan had told his family nothing of what Liz Gordon had said. He hadn't told anybody, except Simon.

'Bain was alive two days before we found him,' he said. 'And in those two days he not only died, he was reduced to a skeleton as well. Liz Gordon says there's a big cover-up going on, because people might get scared if they knew the truth.'

Mrs Hanley stacked dishes in the sink, turned on the tap and squirted washing-up liquid into the water. She looked round at her son.

'Are you making this up, Tan?' Anne folded the paper and stood up. 'Of course he is. I'm off to watch TV.' She left the kitchen.

'No, I'm not!' Tan pushed back his chair. 'Why does nobody ever believe me? Anybody'd think I didn't know how to tell the truth.' He got up and stood with his hands in his pockets, looking out of the window. His mother looked at his back.

'Well,' she said. 'It does sound a bit unlikely, Tan, doesn't it? I mean, if what you say is true, why hasn't one of the big papers got hold of it, or the telly? It's not easy to keep things quiet these days, you know.'

'I don't know. All I know is what I've told you. There's something funny going on that people don't know about. One of these days it'll all

110

come out and then perhaps you'll believe me. If we're not all skeletons by then of course.'

'Ooh Tan – don't!' His mother shivered and pulled on rubber gloves. 'Come and wipe for me, there's a love.' She turned to the sink. Tan sighed, grabbed a tea-towel and picked up a steaming plate.

They were doing the last bits when Anne came through to the kitchen looking peculiar.

'Mum,' she said. 'There's just been a horrible item on TV. You know that chicken farm you pass on the way to Pinfold?' Mrs Hanley nodded. 'I know it, love, but I'm not sure I want to hear.'

'I want to,' said Tan. His sister shot him a withering glance. Their mother sighed. 'Go on, dear: what about the chicken farm?'

'It's been raided,' said Anne. 'Something got into two of the sheds and killed a thousand chickens. The farmer was nearly crying.'

'Foxes I expect,' said Mrs Hanley, slotting a plate into the drainer. 'They kill for fun, you know. Far more than they can eat.'

'No.' Anne shook her head. 'That's the horrible thing about it, Mum. They've ruled out foxes. In the first place the sheds were fox-proof, and in the second these birds *were* eaten – every one. When the farmer went in this morning there were only bones and feathers.'

'Could it have been rats?'

'No. The interviewer suggested that. The farmer said rats will kill a few birds and

111

maim others, but nothing like this. And anyway the door catches were off. It's as though some*body* did it, not some *thing*. The police are investigating but so far it's a complete mystery.'

Tan picked up a fistful of cutlery. 'There you are,' he said. 'I told you there was something funny going on, didn't I?'

'Oh, Tan!' His mother looked at him. 'You surely don't believe this has anything to do with poor Bain. That farm's miles away. It's a coincidence, that's all.'

'I don't believe in coincidences,' growled Tan. 'You just watch: I bet we never find out what happened to those chickens, because it's the same thing that happened to Bain.'

'Rubbish!' cried Anne. 'You've got an over-ripe imagination, Tan. You think the world's full of plots and conspiracies and mysterious happenings and it's not.'

'Isn't it?' He crashed cutlery into the drawer. 'You should talk to a milkman I met the other day, then.'

'Now that'll do, you two!' Their mother spoke sharply, pulling out the plug and draping its chain across the taps. 'Whatever's going on, it's none of our business and they'll tell us when they want us to know.' She peeled off her gloves. 'Tim'll be here soon, Anne. And I expect your animals want seeing to, Tan.'

Anne looked at her watch, let out a little yelp and ran for the stairs. Tan slammed the cutlery drawer, hung up the tea-towel and went out to the shed. An idea was forming in his mind and he wanted to think.

2 1

Simon came round at half-past seven. He knew Tan would be in the shed. He knocked and walked in. Tan had finished his work and was sitting on the bench.

'Hi,' said Simon. 'How's the expectant mother?'

'Sssh!' Tan glanced past his friend. 'I haven't told my mum yet. Shut the door.' Simon did so. Tan smiled. 'She's OK. Fatter than ever.' The smile faded. 'I want to talk to you about something.'

Simon shrugged. 'Well – here I am. What is it?'

'Come and sit down.'

Simon joined Tan on the bench. The animals made soft rustlings in the half-light. He looked sideways at his friend. 'Well – what's up?'

Tan picked at the rough wood between his knees. 'There's something going on,' he said.

'How d'you mean?'

'Well.' Tan peeled a long splinter from the

bench and began cleaning his nails with it. 'You know I told you Bain became a skeleton in two days?'

'Yes.'

'And you remember that cat we found and you kept its skull for your collection?' The other boy nodded.

'And I saw all those mice the other day?'

'Uh-huh?'

'Well – I think the mice have got something to do with Bain and the cat.'

Simon looked at him. 'The mice? You mean you think mice killed them? You're crazy, Tan.'

'I knew you'd say that. Did you see that bit on the telly about the chicken farm?'

'Yes.'

'A thousand chickens reduced to skeletons. Skeletons, Simon. Does that remind you of something?'

'Yes . . . ' Simon gazed at his swinging feet. 'But the doors were fastened. Somebody opened them. Mice couldn't do that.'

'I know. That's the snag.' Tan put the splinter between his teeth and chewed it. After a moment he said, 'I ran away from them, Simon. I didn't tell you that.' His friend looked at him.

'Why did you run?'

Tan shrugged. 'They scared me. There were so many of them and they seemed to sneak up on me.'

'Mice don't crash through the undergrowth

115

at the best of times,' said Simon. 'It doesn't mean they're sneaking up.'

'I know. But what are they doing there in the first place? Doesn't it strike you as odd that there's suddenly loads of white mice on the Tangle?'

Simon nodded. 'It's odd, yes, but they can't have anything to do with Bain, or that cat. Or the chickens, come to that. Mice don't kill people, and they don't undo door catches either.'

'Hmm.' Tan plucked the splinter from his mouth, examined the chewed end and flicked it spinning across the shed. 'I suppose you're right, Simon. As usual. But something's going on for sure, and I wouldn't mind getting to the bottom of it. Come on.'

They left the shed. In its makeshift cage the pregnant female moved heavily to and fro, putting the finishing touches to the nest it had made for its young.

2 2

It was Tuesday of the first week in May. Simon and Tan were walking home from school. Two weeks had passed since the chicken farm incident. The police had issued a statement saying somebody had forgotten to close the shed doors and rats had got in. There had been a piece about it in the Gazette.

Tan said, 'It's funny, isn't it – first they say rats don't work like that, then they say it was rats after all. D'you fancy a look at the Tangle?'

Simon shook his head. 'No thanks. I promised. And besides, I don't like it – not since Bain and all that. Nobody goes there now except a few big kids. What the heck d'you want to go there for?'

Tan shrugged. 'I don't know. I suppose I'm still thinking about the mice. Nothing ever happened in Market Fulford till we found that body. Market Dullford. Then suddenly it's the mystery centre of the western world. I feel like a poke around, that's all.'

117

'Well, you'll have to poke without me,' said Simon firmly. 'I wouldn't go through that fence now if you paid me. I'll see you tonight then?'

They were approaching the hole in the fence. Tan nodded. 'Come about seven. The baby mice are moving around a bit now.'

Simon nodded. 'Have you told your mother yet?'

'No. I don't know how to.'

'Chicken.'

'Chicken yourself. At least I dare go on the Tangle.' He flipped a hand at his friend and ducked through the gap. Simon walked on.

Twenty metres behind, in the shadow thrown by the fence, Gary Deacon saw the two boys part and smiled.

2 3

He went down the slope, swishing through fresh grass and the green spikes of willow-herb. The police had worn a path here a month ago with the frequency of their passing, yet so rank were the weeds that it had gone, like a wound miraculously healed. Tan reached the bottom and turned right.

Bain. It was funny how everything had gone quiet. Liz Gordon had been dead right about that. The police must have asked her editor not to print anything which might arouse public concern and he hadn't. As far as the people of Market Fulford were concerned a body, not a skeleton, had been found in Low Grange Tunnel and investigations into how it came to be there were continuing. Tan hadn't seen the reporter since the night she'd picked him up. How was she coping with her secret? She wasn't the sort of person who would happily keep quiet about a thing like that.

119

As he approached the tunnel, Tan slowed down. He had been walking with his hands in his pockets, deep in thought. Now he began looking about him carefully as he walked. There was a tingling sensation at the back of his neck and a feeling as though he was being watched. He shook his head to dispel the sensation.

'Look at you,' he hissed in self-mockery. 'Four in the afternoon, blazing sunshine and you're chicken, just like Simon said.' He pressed forward, determined not to be scared off. His eyes swept the undergrowth but there was no sign of mice. He was within a couple of paces of the tunnel when Deacon sprang from behind a clump of elders and barred his way.

'Now then, Hanley,' growled the bully. 'I thought I told you to keep off my patch. What you doing anyway – looking for another body or something?'

Tan gazed at the bigger boy. His face was expressionless but his mind raced. They were alone, the two of them. No witnesses. There was no telling what Deacon might do.

'I didn't expect to see you, Deacon.' He forced himself to speak calmly. 'I thought they'd have picked you up at school.'

Deacon scowled. 'What d'you mean, picked me up at school? Who?'

'The police,' said Tan. 'They came to school today. Asked what I was doing in the tunnel

120

the day I found the body. I had to tell 'em you trussed me up and dumped me in there. They seemed interested. I thought maybe they reckoned it could be you put Bain in there too, and I thought they'd have questioned you by now. They will: you could tell by their faces.'

Deacon's face had paled visibly. His jaw sagged and he plucked distractedly at the zipper on his jacket. 'I didn't put Bain in there,' he croaked. 'I never seen Bain in my life.'

Tan shrugged. 'Never said you did, Deacon.'

'No, but you split on me about that other thing though, didn't you? Put me under suspicion when you knew I never laid a finger on Bain.' His voice broke and Tan knew he was close to panic. He pressed home his advantage.

'They're looking for you, Deacon,' he said. 'That's for sure. And I wouldn't let 'em find you here if I were you: not right at the scene of the crime, as they say.'

'Crime?' The big boy's eyes grew wild as he glanced about him. 'There wasn't no crime. You know that. You'll tell 'em, won't you, Hanley? You'll tell 'em old Gary's no killer, eh?'

Tan gazed levelly at the disintegrating bully and said nothing. Deacon stood for a moment, biting his lip and twisting the zipper. Then he whirled and ran, bounding away up the far slope with astonishing speed.

Tan followed the lout with his eyes till, with

a leap and a scrabbling of boots, he disappeared over the two-metre wall.

Then he let out a long sigh and shook his head. He was safe now, but he didn't feel good. He'd lied to save his skin and maybe he'd had no choice, but it had been a rotten trick and he knew it. Now he felt sorry for Gary Deacon. The lad was clearly terrified and probably would not go home tonight. He might even run away altogether: leave Market Fulford and lose himself in London or something. Tan wished he'd gone home with Simon.

He stood for perhaps a minute, gazing absently towards the wall. Then he became aware that the eerie sensation he'd felt before was returning. He glanced into the tunnel, shivered and began hurrying back the way he had come. He didn't run. He simply hurried with a cold tingling in his neck, along the bottom and then left up the overgrown track towards the fence.

He crossed the road and made his way along to the park, feeling faintly sick. It was teatime, but there were people in the park. He found a bench and sat on it, breathing deeply. The cool air and the people made him feel better. He shook his head.

'I'm going daft,' he murmured. 'I must be. I handle Deacon, then run away from nothing.'

He sat for a while, then got up and walked slowly home.

24

It was well after midnight but Tan couldn't sleep. He lay staring at the ceiling of his room, pondering the events of recent weeks. His mother had called it coincidence and Simon had told him mice don't open doors, but it still wouldn't leave him alone. His body under the covers was damp with sweat and his head ached. For the hundredth time he found himself going back over the things that had happened, searching for something that might either confirm or disprove the half-formed idea that haunted him.

The mice. No matter what anybody said, it had all started with finding those mice. Before that everything had been all right but straight after, odd things had begun to happen. The other animals had seemed frightened of the mice. Simon, a level-headed lad who was going to be a scientist, had suddenly become scared and had taken his mice back to the Tangle. And Tan himself had felt uneasy that night. He'd almost released his own mice too, only he'd made himself hang on to see what happened.

Then there was the cat's skeleton, and Bain. Bain, reduced to rags and bones in two days. A rag and bone man. Tan shivered. There had been his encounter with the creatures last Friday, and then the milkman's ghost. He couldn't see how the so-called ghost fitted into the picture. The milkman had seen something two metres tall. He was probably insane or something, but it was one more incident connected with the Tangle.

And now the chicken farm. Rats, said the police. No, said the voice in Tan's head. No way. Not after the farmer himself had said rats don't operate like that. What, then? Mice that can open doors? Ought he to go to the police and share his theory with them? He could just see it.

'What can we do for you, son?'

'I know who killed Bain.'

'Oh aye: who?'

'Mice.'

'Are you trying to be funny, lad?'

'No. They killed a cat too, and a thousand chickens.'

'OK Spiderman – that's enough, unless you want me to come round and see your dad.'

'And they scared my gerbils and chased me away from Low Grange Tunnel.'

'FROG OFF!'

That's how it would go. Something like that. And he knew he wouldn't get anywhere telling his parents either. They thought he was daft enough already. They'd probably have him put away. If he had something definite it'd be different, but he didn't. He had no evidence to offer – no proof of any sort. There was just this daft idea that wouldn't let him sleep.

All right then. He sat up, punched his pillow into a plump shape, and sank on to his side. Proof. That was the next thing. Proof that there was something strange about the white mice. Or that there wasn't. He had seven of them in the shed. Two adults, five babies. He'd watch them. Observe their behaviour in a scientific manner. Make notes, perhaps. Simon might help – it was his sort of thing.

Beyond the dark window a wind had sprung up. Drizzle hissed against the pane. He got a mental picture of Gary Deacon in a country lane somewhere, trudging through the night in sodden clothes. He groaned and rolled over, pulling the covers over his head. He made himself imagine a barnful of hay, and Deacon walking towards it. He watched as the lout went inside and began burrowing his way into the warm, sweet hay. He watched him fashion a snug chamber for himself, right in the middle of the stack, and felt how the warmth seeped into his bones.

He slept.

25

It was Saturday before Tan managed to see Simon alone. They met in the park. A chill mist hid the sun and the place was deserted. Diane had gone off with her parents to a flea-market somewhere. The boys sat on damp swings and Tan told his friend what had happened on the Tangle. When he'd finished, Simon shrugged. 'I told you to keep away from there, didn't I?'

Tan nodded. 'Look, Simon,' he said. 'I can't get this mouse-thing out of my mind. I was awake for hours the other night. There is something funny about them, and I'm going to find out what it is.'

Simon regarded him quizzically. 'How?'

'By watching them.'

'D'you mean you're going to hang about near the tunnel?'

Tan shook his head. 'No, you twit! I'm talking about my mice – the ones at home. The babies are growing up now. I've put 'em all back in the one cage and I'm watching them.'

126

'You've put the two adults together?'

Tan nodded.

'Your mum'll go mad,' cried Simon. 'What if they have more babies?'

Tan shrugged. 'Who's going to know? Nobody goes in there except me. Will you help me, Simon?'

'Your mum'll know there's something going on if she sees me hanging around all the time. Why don't you tell your parents, or the police?'

Tan shook his head. 'You're joking. They'd have me in a padded cell. Besides, the Famous Five don't go running to the police. Not till right at the end. They handle everything themselves.'

Simon snorted. 'You and your Famous Five. There aren't many dead bodies in their adventures, Tan. If what you suspect is right, which it isn't, then it's a deadly serious matter, and deadly serious matters aren't resolved by kids on their own – not in real life they're not.'

Tan nodded. 'OK. Only I can't go to anybody because I've got no proof. I'm asking you to help me get proof. Will you do it?'

Simon studied the beads of moisture on the chain of his swing. 'I think you're barmy,' he said quietly. 'But I'll watch the mice with you if you want. I won't go on the Tangle though, and if we did find anything, I'd want to go straight to the police. OK?'

Tan nodded. They swung for a while, then left the park and went to Tan's house.

2 6

The mice behaved like mice. The two boys spent most of that weekend watching the creatures without noticing anything unusual. On Sunday Tan spoke to Diane and she told him he was crazy. Simon said, 'There you see – isn't that just what I've been saying? If she thinks you're crazy, what chance would you have with an adult?' It was as much as Tan could do to persuade his friend not to abandon the experiment.

They went on watching, every evening after school. One teatime Mrs Hanley said, 'Tan – what are you and Simon up to in that shed?'

'We're training a gerbil to do tricks,' Tan lied. 'Simon has this guinea-pig that can stand on its head and walk a tightrope and play soccer and answer the phone. When we've trained the gerbil, we're going to teach one of the mice and then we'll have a miniature circus. There'll be performing fleas too, if Anne will lend us some of hers.'

'Aw, funny!' sneered Anne. 'You won't have

to look far for a clown either, will you?'

'Oh, stop it, you two!' said their mother. Mr Hanley glared at them over his teacup, and that was the end of the matter. It was about a week after that that a woman called Mrs Lazenby saw the ghost.

27

It was in the Gazette. Mr Hanley was reading the paper after tea. Suddenly he let out a snort and said, 'Silly season's early this year.'

'What d'you mean, dear?' asked his wife. Tan, on his way out to the shed, paused by the living-room door.

'Well, just listen to this.' Mr Hanley folded the paper, adjusted his glasses and read. 'Char's Dust-Up With A Phantom.' He paused to let this witty headline sink in, then continued.

'Office cleaner Mrs Joyce Lazenby turned whiter than white early today when she bumped into a ghost on the streets of Market Fulford. The incident happened at five-fifteen a.m. near the junction of Grange Road and Fairfield Street. Mrs Lazenby was walking along Grange Road in the direction of Rutherford Park when she saw a white figure coming at her out of the mist. "It was horrible," she told our correspondent. "It was moving really fast out of Fairfield

Street and I didn't see it till the last minute because of the mist. It came straight at me. I tried to dodge out of the way but I wasn't quick enough and it bumped me as it passed. I fell down, and by the time I'd picked myself up it had crossed the road and vanished." Mrs Lazenby described the figure as being about two metres tall and "shapeless". She insisted that it moved soundlessly and could only have been a ghost. "There's that old story about the railwayman," she said. "I've always taken it with a pinch of salt but I believe it now." A police spokesman said he was not aware of any similar incidents in the vicinity, and thought that Mrs Lazenby could have been deceived by the mist. "It was probably a large dog," he said.'

Mr Hanley tossed the paper on to the settee. 'Daft,' he growled. 'Can't be much news about if they've got to print stuff like that.'

Mrs Hanley disagreed. 'Some people like to read about such things, dear. Relieves the monotony, I expect.'

'I'd rather be bored than read rubbish,' said Anne. Tim was on duty and she was in a bad mood. Tan said nothing. The story had given him an odd feeling in his stomach and he left the room looking thoughtful.

'There can't be any connection, you loony!' said Simon. 'Mice don't grow two metres tall.'

'No,' agreed Tan. 'She must have seen something, though, and it fits in with that milkman's tale. What d'you reckon they saw – the actual ghost?'

'Don't talk wet!' Simon had his glasses off and was polishing them with a Kleenex. 'There are no ghosts. It was probably a dog like the policeman said.'

'Two metres high?'

'Well, no,' admitted Simon. 'But it was misty, remember. Perhaps it was a stray pony.'

'Or a yak,' suggested Tan. 'Or even a kangorillapig.'

'Twit!' Simon held his glasses up with both hands and squinted through them with tiny, screwed up eyes. Satisfied, he slipped them on and tried to stuff the Kleenex down the back of Tan's neck. There was a brief scuffle and the tissue fell to the floor.

They separated, laughing. Tan straightened his collar. Simon said, 'Tan – I think you're wrong about this.'

Tan looked at him. 'About what?'

'This business of the mice. We've sat here days watching them and they just behave like mice. Don't you think it might be coincidence, those things happening like that?'

Tan shook his head. 'You saw what they did to your guinea-pigs,' he said. 'They scared 'em to death and you let them go. And you've been trying to persuade me to release mine ever since.'

Simon nodded. 'I know, but I think it's only that they're wild, Tan. We're sitting here cooped up when we could be out playing. It seems – oh, I don't know – a waste of time I suppose. You should have let 'em go in the first place.'

'But if they're dangerous,' Tan protested, 'surely it's our duty to . . . ' He broke off and glanced sharply across at the mouse-cage. The animals sat in a huddle close to the bars – so close that four or five quivering noses protruded. The creatures had crowded into so small a space that they were piled on one-another's backs and in the dim light, Tan had the momentary impression of a single, many-eyed animal the size of a kitten.

He nudged his friend. 'Look!'

The mice began to separate. Simon frowned. 'Look at what?'

'That,' said Tan. 'Didn't you see? They clump together now and then. I've noticed it a few times but I wanted you to see for yourself.'

'So they clump together,' said Simon. 'So what?'

'Do all mice do that?' asked Tan.

Simon shrugged. 'Dunno. That's the trouble, you see. We sit here waiting for 'em to do something abnormal, but we don't know what's normal and what isn't. I mean, they'd have to start talking or playing guitars or something before we'd know. What were you going to say about this clumping lark, anyway?'

Tan chewed his lip. Simon waited. After a while he said, 'What if they went about like that?'

Simon glanced sidelong at him. 'How d'you mean?'

'Well: suppose there's a lot of mice. Twenty or thirty of them, and there's this cat that terrorizes them. Sneaks up when they're in the open and nabs one now and then. If they're ordinary mice there's nothing they can do about it, but if they can clump together and sort of roll along like that, they'll be bigger than the cat, won't they?'

'You're crazy.'

'Maybe,' said Tan, quietly. 'I saw this cartoon once, in a book. I remembered it the other night when I couldn't sleep. It was in two parts. The first picture showed a tiny little fish being chased by a bigger one. The big fish had its mouth open and the little one looked scared to death. In the second picture a whole lot of tiny little fish had formed themselves into a shoal that was shaped like one enormous fish, and they were chasing the big fish.'

Simon stared across the shed. 'You're crazy, Tan,' he whispered. 'I ought not to be here alone with you. You might attack me or something.'

'Go if you want,' said Tan. 'Only let me finish first. I couldn't think what was significant about that cartoon – why I'd thought of it just then. Then I remembered how I'd noticed the mice clumping together and it all started falling into place.' He looked at the other boy. 'Can't you see how it might explain things?'

Simon nodded. 'Yes, but it's impossible, Tan.'

Tan shook his head. 'No, it's not. Not if you remember the falling star.'

2 8

Simon stared at Tan. 'Falling star?'

Tan nodded. 'Yes. You remember. Last autumn. It fell on the Tangle, only I don't think it was a falling star.'

'What was it, then?' There was a horrid fascination about his friend's bizarre invention: a fascination which held Simon in spite of himself.

'I think it was some sort of craft,' said Tan. 'A spacecraft. I don't think these things are mice at all. I think they're from space.'

Simon stared at his companion. 'You've flipped your lid,' he gasped. 'You can't really believe all this stuff. Where's your evidence, for heaven's sake?'

Tan made a wry face. 'There is no evidence. That's the trouble. That's why I haven't told anybody. There's loads of little bits that fit together but not a single thing we could take to the police. I don't know what the heck to do, Simon.'

Simon stared at the floor. 'What are some of the bits, Tan?'

'How d'you mean?'

'The bits that fit together. What are they?'

'Well.' Tan paused, frowning. Then he began speaking rapidly, ticking off points on his fingers as he made them.

'One: this thing, whatever it is, falls on the Tangle. We go looking for it and Diane sees something in the tunnel. Something white.

'Two: we come across a cat's skeleton.

'Three: we find baby mice in the mattress.

'Four: there's Bain in the tunnel, picked clean in no time.

'Five: I see hundreds of mice on the Tangle. They don't run away: I do.

'Six: this milkman sees something white. He thinks it's a ghost but there are no ghosts, so it's white and it goes on the Tangle. It could be mice, except it's two metres tall.

'Seven: Mrs Lazenby also sees something white she suspects is a ghost.

'Eight: we watch these mice here. They clump together into something the size of a kitten. If there were hundreds they might be two metres tall.

'Nine: someone or something raids that chicken farm. Skeletons again, like Bain and the cat. Mice don't open doors, you said. But what about a mountain of mice two metres high? Or three? Or four?'

'Now hang on a minute!' interrupted Simon. 'Operating door catches isn't just a matter of being tall enough. You've got to know how as well. That's why cows can't get out of fields – they can reach the latch on the gate but they never learn how to open it.'

Tan's eyes narrowed. 'Listen, Simon,' he hissed. 'A cow's got a great big body and a tiny little brain, right? Seven hundred mice have seven hundred brains. Suppose they link brains as well as bodies when they go into a clump: what then?' He sat forward, his hands gripping the edge of the bench between his knees and stared intently at his companion.

Simon's face was pale. He gazed across at the mouse-cage, biting his lip. After a while he said, 'OK, Tan. It fits and it's convincing. It's fantastic as well but I think it might be just enough to make an adult want to investigate. The question is, would anybody listen? We need something to show 'em, like one of these things opened up.'

'Opened up?'

Simon nodded. 'If they're not mice they'll be different inside. We could get somebody to dissect one – somebody who knows about mice. There's got to be somebody like that up at the Tech.'

'Oh sure!' said Tan. 'We take a mouse up to the Tech. and say, "Cut this up for us will you: it's a space-monster." They'd have us in the loony-bin.'

Simon shrugged. 'Tell your dad, then.'

Tan smiled twistedly. 'You're joking.'

'No I'm not. If you're so sure, tell him. There's hundreds of those things in Low Grange Tunnel and they're breeding all the time. If you're right, they probably killed Bain and they might easily have killed that woman too – that Mrs whats-her-name: Lazenby. I'm not saying I'm totally convinced, Tan, but I think it's time we got it sorted out, one way or the other. Surely your dad will listen when he sees how worried you are?'

Tan shook his head. 'I don't know, but I'll fetch him if you think I should. I don't know what else to do. Wait here.'

He crossed reluctantly to the house, half-hoping that his father would be out.

2 9

'What on earth are you talking about, lad?' Mr Hanley stood in front of the mirror, knotting his tie.

'The mice,' said Tan. 'We think they're dangerous. They clump together and attack things. We don't know what to do.'

'Clump together?' Mr Hanley sat down on the bed and bent to tie his shoelaces. 'What sort of daft trick are you up to now, Tristan – can't you see I'm trying to get ready?' He stood up, shrugged himself into a jacket and tugged it down at the back, looking at his son in the mirror.

'Come to the shed, Dad, please!' cried Tan. 'It'll only take a minute and it's terrifically important. Everybody's in danger if we don't do something.'

'Are they really?' Mr Hanley smiled tightly. 'And all because of a couple of mice, eh? April first's been and gone, lad.' He walked out on to the landing and down the stairs, Tan followed.

His mother was watching television. Mr Hanley said, 'Do you know what this lad's up to, Myra?' She looked up, glancing from one to the other. 'Why – what's he been saying?'

'Some nonsense about his mice. Dangerous he says. Wants me to go to the shed.'

Tan looked at his mother. 'Please, Mum,' he said. 'It'll only take a minute. Will *you* come, then?'

Mrs Hanley sighed and started to get up. 'No,' said her husband. 'You sit down. I'll go.' He looked at Tan. 'But it had better not be one of your barmy tricks old lad!'

Tan led his father out through the kitchen. Simon was by the shed door. 'Hello Simon,' grunted Mr Hanley. 'Didn't know you were here. What's all this nonsense, eh?'

'I – I don't think it's nonsense, Mr Hanley,' stammered Simon. 'We think someone ought to look into it.' He had always felt a little scared of Tan's father, who spoke in a brusque way and spent little time with his son. Now he brushed past Simon and stood blinking in the dimness of the shed. The boys exchanged glances and followed him in.

'They go into a huddle, Dad,' said Tan. 'And we think ... '

'Hold on a minute!' His father peered into the cage, then at Tan. 'I thought you had two mice in here, not ten. Where'd this lot come from, eh?'

'They had babies,' said Tan lamely. 'And there's only seven.'

His father's face reddened with anger. 'Only seven? There wouldn't be seven if you'd kept 'em apart as you were told. You've been breeding them, haven't you? Lying to your mother about miniature circuses and telling me you don't know what to do. Well, lad, I know what to do. Here!' He seized the cage, turned and pushed past his son. He strode down the garden, tore open the cage and shook it. The mice tumbled out and vanished into the lupins and delphiniums.

The boys stood dumbly watching. Mr Hanley came back up the path and handed the empty cage to Tan. 'No more mice,' he snapped. 'Ever – d'you hear?'

Tan nodded, holding the cage against his chest. His father cast a scowling glance at Simon, then strode rapidly along the path and out through the gateway.

Simon ran his tongue along his lip. His face was white. 'I – I'm sorry, Tan,' he whispered. 'I didn't know he'd be like that about it or I wouldn't have suggested . . . '

'It's OK,' broke in Tan. 'He's moody, that's all. What do we do now?'

Simon shrugged. 'I don't know. We've nothing to show now but I still think we should tell somebody. Let's sleep on it.' He forced a wan smile. 'If we can.'

30

Let's sleep on it, Simon had said, but Tan
couldn't. He'd rolled about so much that the
bedclothes were rumpled and lumpy.

He'd tried talking to his mother after Simon
went home but it was no use. She'd been hurt
and disappointed in him because he'd put the
mice in one cage. She said he'd broken a promise
and she wasn't surprised his father was angry.
She cut him short when he tried to tell her
that the mice weren't mice at all.

'You've let me down, Tan,' she said. 'Now
please don't make it worse by telling me
ridiculous stories.'

He'd gone to bed. He'd heard Anne come in,
then his father. They'd all gone to bed ages
ago but he still couldn't sleep.

I still think we should tell somebody, Simon
had said. But who? It's easy in books or on TV.
It always works out all right there, but what
do you do when you think something awful is
happening and everybody thinks you're daft?

143

Everybody? For some reason Liz Gordon's face floated into his mind and he felt a stab of excitement. Liz Gordon wasn't like everybody else. Maybe if he went to her she'd listen. If I can do you a favour sometime, be sure and call me. She'd said that.

The more he thought about it the more sure he became that Liz would listen. He smiled in the dark. 'I'll do it,' he whispered. 'I'll go tomorrow, straight from school.' He felt better already. A trouble shared is a trouble halved. He drifted off to sleep.

Simon wasn't asleep. Like Tan he'd lain awake for hours. Unlike Tan, he had somebody he could go to when he wanted to talk in the night. They'd done it hundreds of times, Diane and himself: crept into each other's rooms for whispered conversations in the small hours. Nobody knew.

'It still sounds crazy to me,' whispered Diane, hugging her knees. Simon was sitting on the edge of her bed. He nodded. 'I know, but Tan made it sound so convincing. You should have been there. We've got to at least get somebody to investigate. The trouble is, nobody will listen. You should have seen Tan's dad tonight.'

'Last night,' corrected Diane, glancing at the clock-radio. 'It's half-past one.' She yawned. 'That idea about taking a mouse up to the Tech was best.'

144

'I know,' growled Simon. 'But it's no use saying that now. We haven't got one.'

'Get one,' said Diane.

Simon looked at her. 'Where?'

'The Tangle. You said there were hundreds there. Go and catch one.'

'Not likely!' He shivered. 'Look what happened to Bain.'

Diane shrugged. 'You won't get anyone to believe you then, will you?' She yawned again and said, 'Look – can we talk about it tomorrow? I'm shattered.'

'So'm I.' He stood up and stretched. 'P'raps I'll sleep, now that I've worn myself out. G'night.'

'G'night.' She watched him steal away, then sat with her chin on her knees and her eyes closed. She still didn't believe Tan's tale, but it was hard to think of a better explanation for recent events.

'Well,' she told herself presently, 'there's only one way to find out – somebody's got to get hold of a specimen and it looks as though it'll have to be me.' She snuggled down and pulled up the covers.

'I'll go to the Tangle,' she whispered. 'Tomorrow. Straight after school.'

3 1

Diane loitered in the cloakroom till the other girls had gone. She checked her satchel to make sure the empty chocolate-box was there. It was. She would dawdle along the road and reach the Tangle after her friends had passed it. With any luck she'd be away before the Comp came out.

It was a fine afternoon. The sun felt warm on her arms and face and she hummed softly to herself as she strolled along. It was hard to believe that there was anything sinister lurking nearby. In fact she didn't believe it. Not now, with the birds singing and the sun shining. She'd been half-persuaded, sitting there with Simon in the dark, but then weird things are believable at night. She was sure now that the mice were only mice. She'd catch one to prove it, and later they'd have a good laugh about the whole thing.

There was nobody on the Tangle. There hardly ever was, these days. Diane made her way down the slope and walked towards the tunnel. As she walked she undid her satchel and turned back the flap. She wanted the chocolate-box handy. She scanned the long grass beside the track, hoping to surprise a mouse in the open. She'd given up hope of doing so when she spotted one, flitting between the stems. She gave chase.

If the creature had turned aside she would have lost it in the undergrowth, but it didn't. Instead it ran out on to the bare, shaly patch and she pursued it eagerly. She didn't look up. If she had, she might have realized that the mouse was leading her straight towards the mouth of the tunnel.

3 2

As Diane left school on her way to the Tangle, Tan was boarding the bus which would drop him outside the offices of the Market Fulford Gazette. At ten to four he walked into the front office and asked to see Liz Gordon. The receptionist, a plump lady with blue hair, eyed him suspiciously.

'What's it about, dear?'

'It's personal,' Tan told her.

The woman sniffed. 'Really? Miss Gordon knows you, then?'

Tan nodded. 'We've worked together.'

'Hmm. What's your name?'

'Tan. Tan Hanley.'

The woman frowned. 'Tan? What sort of a name is that?'

'A rotten one,' Tan replied. 'It's short for Tristan.'

'I see. Well: if you'd care to wait I'll tell Miss Gordon you're here.'

The woman went into her cubby-hole and picked up a phone. Tan leaned on the counter. 'Newsroom please,' said the receptionist. She stood on one foot and examined her long, scarlet fingernails. After a moment she said, 'Reception. Visitor for Miss Gordon. A boy: Tristan Hanley.' A pause, then 'Certainly. Thank you.' She hung up and came out, wearing an artificial smile. 'Miss Gordon will see you, dear,' she said. 'Take the lift to the third floor.'

Liz was waiting when he stepped out of the lift. 'Hello, Tan,' she smiled. 'This is a pleasant surprise.' She stuck out her hand and Tan took it, blushing furiously. 'I – wanted to see you,' he stammered, 'About the mice.'

'Mice?' She frowned. 'What mice, Tan?' Before he could answer she said, 'Look – it's a bit noisy in the newsroom. Let's go in here where we can talk.' She steered him into a small, unoccupied office and he sat down. She closed the door and joined him.

'Now then Tan,' she said. 'What's all this about, eh?'

Briefly, Tan told the reporter how they had found the mice in the mattress, and outlined the events of the past weeks. At the beginning he could sense her incredulity. She was ready to laugh at his story, but by the time he'd finished she was grave.

'I know it all sounds daft,' he said. 'But I

149

can't think of any other explanation and I'm scared. I think we should show one of those things to somebody.'

'Yes.' The woman was silent for a while, staring at the carpet. Tan sat with his hands in his lap, watching her. Presently she roused herself.

'Yes,' she said, briskly. 'I think you're absolutely right, Tan. It does sound ridiculous but there's so much circumstantial evidence that it's got to be investigated, and the sooner the better. I don't think the authorities are acting, so we'll have to do it ourselves. D'you think you could catch one of those mice?'

Tan nodded. 'Yes. The thing is, I . . . ' He looked away, biting his lip.

'What is it, Tan?'

He shook his head. 'It's just that the last time I went near that tunnel I was scared to death. Suppose they attack us, Liz? We could end up like Bain.'

'True.' The reporter stood up and smoothed down her skirt. 'But I think we're just going to have to take that chance, Tan. If you're right, somebody's got to do something, and if you're wrong there's no danger. Come on.'

33

The mouse scuttled into the tunnel and Diane followed, the satchel swinging and banging against her side. She was ten metres in before she realized what she was doing. She skidded to a stop. The mouse darted away into the gloom.

Something brushed against her ankle and she flinched. A mouse ran past, followed at once by another. There came a sound like the patter of rain on dry leaves and a fast creamy foam swept out of the darkness like a wave racing in over sand. She turned, screaming, and began running back. The wave overtook her; became a live, furry carpet unrolling before her and she trod on soft, squealing lumps as she ran.

Out of the floor in front of her grew a soft white bulge. It grew outward and upward and became a thousand-eyed bear that loomed, gnashing its countless little teeth.

She screamed and tried to swerve round it but

it knew, before she knew herself, the way that she would go. She started to turn. Something shifted under her shoe so that she fell and they swarmed on her, with their tiny, scampering feet and needle-teeth, and she knew that she would die. She began to shriek.

Through the echo of her screams, she heard her name. Somebody was calling: 'Diane, Diane.' The creatures ran over her face and entangled themselves in her hair. She swatted and clawed and cleared her mouth to cry, 'Here: I'm here!'

Rapid footfalls. Voices. Two silhouettes against the light, one of them wielding something, clubbing and slashing. Tan!

She managed to get up on her knees. The creatures began to let go: dropping from her body and darting away. She knelt in a sea of mice and plucked them off herself, sobbing. A woman came and lifted her to her feet and half-carried her towards the light. She recognized the reporter. They passed Tan, yelling and trampling, wielding a broken stake.

And then they were out in bright sunshine, running. The woman's arm circled Diane's waist and she ran awkwardly, half-sideways, supporting the girl. They climbed the slope, panting. Tan came last, looking back.

'Thank you,' gasped Diane, as the reporter helped her through the gap.

'Never mind that, love,' Liz Gordon replied. 'Here: lean on me.'

They hobbled towards the car. A man stared at them from across the road. Tan came through the gap, saw her looking and held something up. It was her satchel.

3 4

The tyres shrieked as Liz Gordon took a sharp
bend, making for the hospital. Diane clung to
the armrest and closed her eyes. She felt ill,
and hoped she wasn't going to be sick in the
reporter's car. Tan, sitting beside her, squeezed
her arm. Liz half-turned in her seat.

'Did you get one of those things, Tan?' she
asked. Tan nodded, grinning. 'Half a satchel-
ful.' Diane shivered and edged away from the
satchel that lay on the seat between them.

They reached the infirmary. Liz followed the
signs to Casualty, and parked. Diane walked
unsteadily into the building, with Tan on one
side and Liz on the other.

'What're we going to say?' whispered Tan as
they approached the reception-hatch. A severe-
looking woman in rimless glasses was sitting
at the hatch.

'I'll say she was playing with her pet mice
and got bitten,' hissed Liz. 'It's not very good
but we can't possibly tell the truth, and it'll get

her a tetanus-jab.' Diane's clothes were filthy and the receptionist looked sceptical when Liz told her story, but she wrote on a card and told them to go and sit on a bench.

Liz got Diane settled, then turned to Tan. 'Stay with her,' she said. 'And when she's been attended to, take her home in a taxi. Here.' She gave him some money. 'I'm off to the Tech with those mice, if they haven't all escaped.'

'They haven't,' said Tan. 'The live ones are in a chocolate-box with rubber-bands round. The ones in the satchel are dead.'

'OK.' She looked at her watch. 'I'll have to go, or they'll all have gone home. I don't know how you're going to explain to Diane's parents, or yours for that matter, but I'll have to leave that to you. I'll phone in a couple of hours or so, to let you know what's happening. All right?'

Tan nodded. Liz flashed him a smile that made him blush, and left.

She parked in front of the technical college, clattered up the wide marble steps and into the lobby. 'Biology,' she gasped to a startled porter. 'Second floor,' he told her. 'Up the steps and turn right.'

She carried the chocolate-box through some glass doors, up a flight of stairs and along a corridor with a shiny floor. At the end of the corridor a door stood open. As Liz approached, a man in a white coat looked out. 'Hello,' he said. 'Can I help you?'

Liz nodded. 'I hope so: I've got an animal I need dissecting.' She put the box on a window-sill and started to remove the rubber-bands. The man looked at her in surprise.

'We don't dissect for the public,' he said. 'Only for the benefit of our students. Who sent you?'

'Nobody,' Liz told him. 'I'm Liz Gordon from the Gazette. Look.' She held out the box. 'In here are some creatures that look like mice, but aren't. They're alien beings and there's plenty more where these came from. I know you'll think I'm crazy, but believe me this is desperately urgent. I want somebody to look at one: some-body who knows about mice. Do you know about mice?'

The man nodded. 'Yes. I'm a lab. tech. It's part of my job to know a bit about them but it's no part of my job to carry out dissections for anybody who happens to walk in here.'

'Look!' Liz fumbled with the box and raised the lid. 'I want you to look, that's all.' She lifted a mouse out of the box and showed it to the man. He glanced at it and nodded. 'Mouse,' he said. 'Albino. I've got twenty just like it behind that door there.' Liz held the creature out to him.

'Take it!' she cried. 'Take it and have a proper look. If it's a mouse I promise I'll stop pestering you and leave, only look at it properly, please!'

The other mice were trying to get out of the box. She closed the flap and held it down with her free hand.

'Oh, very well.' The man took the creature from her and turned it in his palm. It was clear from his expression that he thought he was humouring a lunatic. He looked at it from various angles and was about to hand it back when he noticed something. He frowned, took one of the tiny forelegs between thumb and finger and peered at it.

'Hmm,' he grunted. 'Odd that. Bit of a claw-thing where no claw-thing ought to be. Some sort of deformity. And here.' He examined the other foreleg. 'The same.' He glanced up peering at Liz over the top of his spectacles. 'You say there are more like this?'

'Yes. Hundreds.'

'Each with this same malformation of . . . '

'I don't know!' cried Liz. 'I haven't examined them, but it's not a malformation. I told you, they're not mice.'

'Hmm. Yes, I know.' Amusement showed in his eyes. 'Alien beings, I believe you said. What makes you say that?'

'They – do strange things,' said Liz. 'Get together in swarms. Build themselves into one big creature with hundreds of eyes. That's what the claw's for, I expect: to help them cling together. They attacked a child, not half-an-hour ago in Low Grange Tunnel. They . . . '

'Yes.' The technician stood for a moment, frowning. Then he said, 'OK. This has got to be some sort of joke, but I'll buy it. It's my teabreak and I wasn't doing anything special. Wait here. I'll pith this fellow and have a look inside, but I'm not expecting anything exciting: nothing exciting at all. Shan't be long.' He went off, whistling tunelessly.

Liz walked into the man's office. There were some steel and canvas chairs. She put the box of mice on a table, sat down and pretended to look at the pin-ups on the wall. She was on edge. She drummed her fingers on the plastic table-top. It seemed a long time before the technician came back.

He was carrying a stainless-steel kidney dish. His face was white and he wasn't whistling.

'It seems you could be right,' he said. 'At least partly. If this is a mouse, it's like no mouse I've ever seen. I'd like to call Doctor Lendall at home and have him come in and look at it.'

Liz had stood up as soon as she'd seen the expression on his face. Now she shook her head impatiently. 'No. I want you to come with me to the police. Tell them what you've just told me. They'll listen to you, where they'd only laugh at me. Tell them these things aren't mice. They'll have to do something then.'

The man gazed at her, biting his lip. He shook his head. 'Sorry,' he said. 'I can't do that. Not on my own authority. It wouldn't do any good anyway: I'm only a technician. If you can get Doctor Lendall to . . . '

'There isn't time!' cried Liz. 'Do you know of any way I could kill them: a disease or something?' The man shrugged.

'Impossible to say. If they were ordinary mice ectromelia might do the trick, but I don't know about these.'

'What's ectromelia?'

'Mouse-pox. It's highly contagious and only affects mice. Makes their legs drop off.'

'Ugh!' Liz shuddered. 'How would I give it to them?'

The technician looked at her. 'A serum. You'd have to inject a few and release them, and they'd pass the infection on to the others.'

'Do you have this serum?'

The man laughed briefly. 'No. It's not kept. You'd need to get it made up.'

'Would you make some up for me?'

He shook his head emphatically. 'Of course not. You don't know what you're asking. Let me call Doctor Lendall.'

Liz made an exasperated gesture. 'There's no time. I tell you. If you won't help, I'll find somebody who will!' She picked up the chocolate-box.

'OK.' The technician shrugged. 'I think you're crazy, but if you're right it's a job for the authorities. You're not going to find anybody who'll make up a serum for you just like that: it's not the way things are done.'

Liz turned in the doorway. 'Listen,' she snarled. 'If I wait for things to be done the way they're usually done, we're going to die: all of us. Thanks for the dissection.' She spun on her heel and clattered away down the corridor. The man gazed after her, shook his head and reached for the telephone.

3 5

Liz Gordon sat in the car. It was five-thirty.
She glanced up at the glass and concrete slab
of the college. That technician would be calling
his boss. Doctor Lendall would probably be here
soon. What he'd do once he'd examined the dead
mouse she didn't know, but if he contacted the
authorities she could be in trouble. She was
pretty certain the police knew more about Bain's
death than they were admitting, and if they
learned that somebody from the press was on
to it, they might try to stop her. She must do
what had to be done, and do it quickly. That
meant getting hold of the ectromelia serum,
but how? From where?

Mice. She drummed with her palms on the
steering-wheel. She needed someone who kept
mice. An expert. Someone who might be more
co-operative than the technician. A breeder.

'Hey!' She exclaimed out loud, slapping the
wheel. A breeder. There was that story about
a breeder, months ago. She'd covered it for

161

the Gazette. This guy bred mice for a living: supplied laboratories all over the country, and he was getting hate-mail. Letters from some organization opposed to animal experiments, threatening to burn his house down and smash his equipment. His place was just a few miles out of town. She'd gone there with a photographer and looked round and done a piece about it: how if there were no animals they'd have to experiment on people. A lot of readers had written in supporting the guy, and the hate-mail had dried up. She smiled.

'He just might reckon he owes me a favour,' she whispered, twisting the key in the ignition. Two minutes later she hit the bypass and put her foot down.

'You can drop us just here,' said Tan. The driver nodded and pulled into the kerb. Tan paid him while Diane got out. The taxi departed and the pair set off up Fairfield Street.

'I thought it'd be easier to arrive at your place on foot,' said Tan. 'I don't think we should say anything about the hospital at all, do you?' Diane shook her head.

'I suppose not.' She looked glum. 'I don't like lying to my parents, Tan. When this is over I'm going to tell them everything.'

'Oh, so am I, when it's over. We've got to keep quiet till Liz has done whatever it is she's doing, though. What're we going to say?'

'I'll say we got caught up in a gang-fight in the playground and got detention. That'll explain the sticking-plaster too.' They had dressed her bites at the hospital.

'Yeah,' Tan nodded. 'That's good. What about Simon, though? He's bound to say, "What gang-fight?" or something.'

They turned a corner. 'If that happens, I'll just have to brazen it out,' said Diane. 'Tell him he must have been round the other side of the school and missed it. I'll manage.'

They reached the Playfairs' gate. Tan looked at her.

'You sure you're all right?' She nodded.

'I'll probably have nightmares and scream the place down, but I'm not going to give the game away if that's what you mean. Be sure and phone us if you hear from Liz, won't you?'

Tan smiled. 'Sure I will. I . . . '

'What?'

He shrugged. 'Nothing. I was going to say I thought girls were supposed to be soft, that's all.'

Liz Gordon knocked on the door. It was opened by a thin, balding man in carpet-slippers.

'Hello, Mr Farnsworth.' The man's eyes widened in surprise.

'Hello: you're the young woman from the paper, aren't you?'

Liz smiled. 'You remember me then. I'm glad

about that, Mr Farnsworth, because I've come
to ask for your help.'

'My help?' The man arched his brow, then
moved to one side. 'You'd better come in,' he
said. 'I was just finishing my tea.'

She followed him into his living room. She
remembered it from the last time. It was a very
neat room and she'd been surprised about that,
because Mr Farnsworth lived alone.

He waved her into a chair, fetched a cup and
saucer and poured her some tea. 'Now then,'
he said. 'How can I help you?'

'Do you know about ectromelia?'

He looked startled. 'I should say so: bane of
my life. But what do you know about it: you
haven't started breeding mice, have you?'

She laughed. 'No, but I need to get rid of some,
and I was told ectromelia's a good way.'

'What?' The man shook his head. 'I don't
know who told you that, love. Ectromelia's
nasty. Traps are what you want, or poison.
Even poison's not as bad as ectromelia.'

Liz sipped her tea. She needed this man's
help, but she knew that if she told him the
whole story, he'd think her insane. She set down
the cup.

'Look, Mr Farnsworth,' she said. 'I'll be honest
with you, as far as I can be. I'm not talking about
a few house-mice or anything like that. If I told
you what was going on you'd say I was mad and
kick me out. What I will say is, I'm talking

about hundreds of mice: thousands, probably. They're all in one place now, but they won't be for long.'

The man opened his mouth to speak but Liz held up her hand. 'I know what you're going to say. Get a pest-control officer in. I can't, Mr Farnsworth; believe me I can't.' She stood up. 'Trust me. This is desperately important. I helped you once, didn't I?' He made no response. 'Didn't I?' He nodded.

'Yes. And I'd like to help you, but I don't understand what you want. Ectromelia's a disease. It's not something in a bottle you can take away with you. What is it you want me to do?'

Liz looked at him. 'I want you to inject a serum of ectromelia into some mice I have in the car.'

The breeder shook his head, sighing. 'There's no such thing,' he said. 'Not here at any rate. I'm sorry.'

The woman thought for a moment. 'Have any of your mice got the disease?' He nodded.

'As it happens, yes. I isolated half a dozen or so only this morning. Why do you ask?'

'Couldn't you draw the virus, or whatever it is, out of them and inject it into mine?'

'I suppose I could,' he replied coldly. 'And I will, if you insist. But I want you to understand that I'll be doing it only because I owe you a favour. It's a heck of a way to kill mice, Miss

165

Gordon: a heck of a way.' He got up, reluctantly, and led her out to the sheds.

Doctor Lendall dialled and drummed his fingers on the desktop. 'Police? This is Doctor Lendall at the Technical College. I want to speak to Superintendent Fisk. Thank you.' He sat back in the swivel-chair. 'Ah, good evening, Superintendent. Look, I'm sorry to be calling at this time. Yes, I was afraid you might be, but something's come up which I think you should know about. You know that P.M. you brought me in on: the Bain thing? Well, somebody came in here an hour ago with a boxful of mice she said she'd found in that tunnel, only they're not mice, Superintendent. I don't know what they are, but I rather suspect they're what ate our friend Bain. Yes, I know it'd take a lot of them: the woman said there are a lot. Hundreds, she told the technician here. She asked him for something to kill 'em off with: a serum. No, of course he didn't. The thing is, she said she was from the Gazette. No, no name, but we don't need three guesses, do we?' He listened for a moment, then grinned. 'Right first time. I'd have a word with her if you intend keeping this thing quiet much longer. Oh, I agree: there'd be mass panic. Yes, I'll come over. She might be an infernal nuisance but she's right about one thing: there's something very odd going on.'

166

* * *

Superintendent Fisk picked up the internal phone. 'Jim: get on to Records. Get that reporter's registration number and alert all patrols. I think we'd better have her in.'

36

'Tan!' His mother called from the house. 'Telephone.'

'Coming, Mum.' He snapped the water-bottle into its clip and left the shed.

'Hello?'

'Tan: Liz Gordon. Listen. I think I've got something that'll fix the mice. If you want to give me a hand, be at the end of Fairfield Street in about ten minutes. How's Diane?'

'Oh, she seemed fine. I'm in the doghouse, though: it was twenty to seven when I got in.'

'I am sorry, Tan. Will you be able to get away?'

'I think so. The others'll want to come too, I reckon.'

'Yes, that's all right. Listen. I've got to go. I'm in a call-box. See you soon.' The phone clicked and he hung up. His mother stuck her head round the kitchen door.

'Who was that, Tan?'

'Liz Gordon. She wants to see me.'

'Oh?' Mrs Hanley came through into the

hallway. 'She's not still bothering you about that dreadful body business, is she?'

Tan nodded. 'It's to do with that, yes. Can I go, Mum, please?'

'Well, I suppose you'll have to,' she said, 'since you've already arranged it. But don't be long: your dad's in a bad enough mood as it is.' Mr Hanley was upstairs changing. He'd been angry when Tan came in late for tea, but his anger had been surprisingly mild, and Tan guessed he was feeling ashamed of yesterday's outburst.

'Thanks, Mum.' He wished he could tell her what was going on. He got his jacket and left.

He hurried to Simon's house. Mr Playfair answered the door.

'Yes, Tan?' His gruffness surprised the boy.

'Could I see Simon please?' he said. Mr Playfair shook his head. 'No, Tan,' he replied. 'I'm afraid you can't. Simon and Diane are in disgrace: they've lied to their mother and broken a promise to me.' He looked at Tan through narrowed eyes. 'Do your parents know you're still visiting that Tangle place?'

Tan gaped. 'How did you . . . ?'

The man snorted. 'Diane's clothes were covered in soot, lad. Whatever happened to her today happened in that filthy tunnel, not at school. And now I think you'd better go: unless of course you've come to tell me the truth.'

'I – can't, Mr Playfair!' cried Tan. 'We have

169

told lies, and broken our promises, but there's a good reason. Can't I just ... '

'Goodbye then, Tan.'

The door closed. Tan stood gazing at it in disbelief. Mr Playfair was a kindly, patient man who spent time with his children and listened to what they had to say. Tan had always considered him aptly named, and had secretly envied his friends. Now, as the man's footfalls receded, it seemed to Tan he'd lost something precious: something he might never have again. He turned and ran down the path.

'What is it, Tan?' The reporter peered at him in the twilight. She had parked in Grange Road and was standing beside the car.

Tan sniffed and shook his head. 'Nothing. It's just – I'm fed-up of telling lies, Liz. I'm in bother at home, and now Mr Playfair's sent me away. I wish I'd never heard of those flipping mice.'

'I know.' She reached out and squeezed his arm. 'With any luck they'll be finished after tonight. Look.' She turned and lifted a small cage out of the car. 'These are the mice you caught, only now they're carrying a deadly disease.'

Tan peered at the creatures. 'They seem all right to me.'

'They're not all right,' Liz told him. 'They've got ectromelia. Now what we do is, we get as close to the tunnel as we dare, and let these fellows go. They'll run to the others and mix with them. Then, every time they go into one of those swarms, they'll pass the disease on. OK?'

Tan shivered. 'I don't fancy going near that tunnel, Liz: it's nearly dark.'

'Yes.' She looked at her watch. 'Ten to nine. It's got to be done, so the sooner we get on with it the better. Come on.'

They paused at the kerb. A car was approaching on sidelights. As it drew near they saw that it was a police car. As it cruised by, the two men inside turned to look at them. Twenty yards away its brake-lights came on and it started to pull in. Liz plucked at Tan's sleeve.

'Listen!' she hissed. 'These guys might be looking for me. Here.' She thrust the cage into his hands. 'Cross over and get through the fence. If they come towards me, run to the tunnel and release the mice. Go!'

The police car was reversing towards them. Tan darted across the road and through the gap in the fence. There he waited, clutching the cage and peering across at the reporter who stood motionless beside her vehicle.

The police car stopped. Both men got out, slammed their doors, and strode towards her. One of them said, 'Miss Gordon?' Tan cursed softly. It was almost dark and he was more scared than he had ever been in his life. He knew they must have seen him standing with the woman. Any second now they'd ask her where he'd gone, and come after him.

171

He turned and looked down the slope. The Tangle lay in shadow. He'd have given anything to be somewhere else – anywhere else. He peeped through the fence. Both policemen had their backs to him. He heard Liz say, 'Boy?' in a surprised voice. He bit his lip, tucked the cage under his arm and set off down the slope.

It wasn't easy in the dark. He stumbled several times, partly because he kept looking back. Nobody was following him. He almost wished they were. He found the track and began walking along it. Fear weakened his joints and he almost fell. He thought of Bain and swallowed hard, biting his lip.

Twenty metres from the tunnel he stopped, straining his eyes.

There was nothing to be seen, but his fear was an invisible barrier across the track and he could go no further. All was silent. Hardly daring to breathe he squatted, opened the cage, and shook out the mice. They sat, darting their heads this way and that. Tan did not watch them. He couldn't. His gaze was riveted on the tunnel. Slowly he straightened up, leaving the cage on the ground. It was quite dark. The mice were pale blobs on the track. They were not moving towards the tunnel. Their motions seemed random: a brief rush, a quivering pause, a rush in another direction. He didn't care.

He turned and began running back. He expected shouts; the flash of a policeman's torch but there was nothing. He glanced back, and saw no wave of speeding froth.

He ran gasping up the slope, making no attempt to move quietly. He had done what the woman had asked. They could do what they liked with him now. He reached the gap and looked through.

The road was deserted. Both cars had gone.

Tan got home at twenty past nine. At half-past, the mice started leaving the tunnel. They poured out like lava from the mouth of a volcano; hundreds and hundreds of them, spreading through the undergrowth till the grass-stems shivered and the Tangle seemed to whisper in the dark.

Nobody saw. If anybody had, he might have thought the creatures moved aimlessly, but they did not. Each individual had its place, and gradually a pattern emerged. The mice were forming groups. Some of the groups were large, others quite small. At ten o'clock a cloudbank covered the moon and the first five hundred slipped away.

3 8

When Tan got home, Tim's car was parked by the gate. He groaned, knowing the young man's presence was going to make his job more difficult. He was going to tell his mother the whole truth and try to enlist her help in getting Liz Gordon released. The reporter must be under arrest or something, and if he could convince his mother that his story was true perhaps she'd do something. He wasn't thinking clearly and he knew it, but with the Playfairs out of the running and now Liz, he didn't know what else he could do. He hurried up the side path and into the kitchen.

His mother was there, making sandwiches for supper. She put down the butter-knife and looked at him.

'Have you seen the time, Tan?' she said. 'I thought I told you not to be long.' Tan nodded.

'I know, Mum,' he said. 'But I couldn't help it. There's something happening: something terrible. I've tried to tell you but you won't listen. Where's Dad?'

'Out,' she told him, flatly. 'As usual. And he wasn't very pleased when I told him you'd gone to meet that reporter. What d'you want him for?'

'I don't,' said Tan. 'I want to talk to you, Mum, on your own. Where are Anne and Tim?'

'In the front room, listening to R.M.F. What's this all about, Tan?'

He looked at her. 'Will you listen properly and not start telling me I'm daft, Mum? It sounds daft, what I'm going to tell you, but it's true. D'you promise?'

She gave him a brief smile. 'All right: I promise. Go on.'

He perched on a stool and told her. He told her everything, while she buttered bread and said nothing. When he'd finished she was slicing salami. She went on slicing it, laying the thin pink discs on the buttered bread, two to a slice. He watched her. After a minute he said, 'Well?'

She sawed away at the salami. 'Well?' she murmured. 'So your friend was taken away by the police, eh? That's what happens to people who meddle in things that don't concern them. It's a wonder they didn't take you away too.'

Tan stared at her. She began smearing mustard on the sandwiches. 'Have – have you been listening to me?' he whispered. His mother smiled faintly.

'Of course, Tan.' She spoke quietly. 'I promised, didn't I? But you see, I don't believe a word of it. Not a single word. Mice are mice. Put that milk-bottle out on the step for me, there's a love.'

He glanced at the empty bottle on the drainer, then back at his mother. She was piling sandwiches on to a plate. 'Mum,' he began. 'I'm not – I'm not a . . . ' He was going to say 'liar' but she interrupted. 'The bottle, Tan. Put it out. And then you can put the kettle on. That young man'll be ready for his supper, I fancy. Come on now!'

He felt an aching lump in his throat. He slid from the stool and took the bottle, keeping his back to her so that she wouldn't see the tears.

He opened the door, put the bottle down on the step and straightened up, wiping the water from his eyes with his knuckles. It was dark. The sky was completely overcast and a warm wind blew spots of rain into his face. He inhaled deeply to ease the ache in his throat. He was turning to go in when he saw something move by the shed.

He saw it for only a moment but it looked like a man. A man in a pale coat who had been standing by the corner of the shed and had drawn back when the boy looked in his direction. He started to call to his mother, then checked himself. No. He wouldn't do that. He'd tried to involve her and she didn't want to know. All right then; he'd manage on his own. He stepped down and crossed the garden, keeping his eye on the spot where the man had disappeared.

He approached the place in a curve, taking it wide so that he would be able to see along the side of the shed without going too close. He only half expected to see anything. The glimpse he thought he'd had might easily have been one of those illusions you sometimes get at night: something moving in the eye-corner that turns out to be nothing at all. He reached a spot from which he could see along the deeply shadowed side and stopped. Something was there. Something tall and pale, dimly seen against the gloom.

His scalp prickled. He held his breath and stood, waiting for the thing to move. There was no sound, except for the wind in the sycamore. After a moment he opened his mouth and called out, 'Who's there?'

There was no answer. The pale shape didn't move. Maybe it wasn't anything after all: reflected light from somewhere, or a bush he'd forgotten was there. He called again, 'Hello?' his voice sounding small in the wind. He crept forward, screwing up his eyes. The shape became neither bush nor man as he drew nearer but remained an amorphous blob in the shadows.

He was within feet of it when it moved. The instant it did so he knew what it was and that really he'd known all along. The swarm came at him like a giant snowman: a nimble snowman, made from eyes and fur and teeth.

For a split-second he froze. The thing loomed, opening like a cloak of fur to wrap him. He whirled and ran, screaming back towards the house.

His mother stood, knife in hand, silhouetted in the doorway. Beside her, pale against the house-wall, a second swarm lay waiting. He swerved, making for the gate. At once, the swarm became a milky flood that raced to cut him off.

He spun, sobbing, and angled back across the garden. Tim was in the doorway now, shouting and waving his arms. 'Help me!' cried Tan. 'I can't keep 'em off any more!'

He was wading through lupins, stumbling into an angle of hedge and fence: a corner from which there was no escape. He turned. Both swarms had swung in behind him and were closing.

Mouth agape, he backed panting into the corner. Dense privet soared above him on his right and the thin, unclimbable rails of the picket-fence stretched away to his left. The swarms closed in, gathering themselves for the final rush.

Between the mice and beyond them he saw Tim Bixby running away down the path. He'd cried out for help and instead of coming to his aid the young man was deserting him.

'All right!' he gasped. 'So I've had it. They'll know they've been in a scrap though!' He bent, pulled a rotten stake from the hedge and waited. The swarms rolled forward, twittering. Somewhere beyond them he heard his mother screaming. The two swarms drew together and merged into a single, charging beast. Tan raised the stake above his head and lashed out.

The rotten wood snapped off near his hand. He flung the stump at the pulsating mass, threw himself back against the fence and wrapped his arms round his head.

Cold droplets spattered his ears and hands. There was a thud and a flash and a searing pain. His sleeve was on fire. He screamed, swatting at it with his hand. A shrill wall of fur and flame heaved about him. His face was scorched. There was a choking smell and when he sucked in breath he ate fire. He twisted away and rammed his face against the fence, gulping air and beating his arm on the rails.

There were shouts and he felt himself seized from behind. He tried to cling to the fence but his head swam and his hands wouldn't grip. He was dragged over backwards and something heavy pinned him to the earth. The pain in his arm intensified and he knew that they were eating it . . . eating it . . .

'Lie still, old chap: doctor's on his way.'

Tan blinked. Tim Bixby's face looked down at him. He couldn't see very well. The light was dim. It flickered on the airman's cheek. He turned his head. He was in the living room. On the settee. There were candles burning on the sideboard. He said, 'What's up with the lights?'

Tim smiled. 'They're out, old lad. Power-cut or something. How d'you feel?'

Tan pulled a face. 'Sick. My arm hurts. Where's Mum?'

'In the kitchen. Want me to fetch her?'

He shook his head. 'No. It doesn't matter. Did she see them: did she see the mice?'

The officer nodded. 'Yes, Tan. She saw them. She's awfully upset because she didn't believe you. She's more concerned about that than anything else in fact. Here she is now.'

His mother knelt down and felt his forehead. Her hand was cool. He smiled at her. 'It's all right, Mum,' he whispered. 'It is a bit far-fetched, isn't it?' She nodded, biting her lip. There were tears on her cheeks. After a moment she said, 'Your dad's gone for the doctor.'

Tan looked at her. 'Gone for him? Why didn't he phone?'

'The phone's out of order,' she said. Tan half-rose, looking for Tim. His mother pushed him gently back into the pillow. 'Lie quietly, love,' she said. 'Your arm's been burned. Tim threw petrol on those – things, and some of it went on you. You've got to lie quietly because of shock.'

181

'I haven't got shock!' cried Tim. 'But we've got to do something. It's not a power-cut and the phone's not out of order. It's them, Mum: they're taking over the town.'

His voice had risen and his mother shushed him. 'I know, Tan. It's all right. Tim's off to alert the armed forces. You've done your share. More than your share.' She shivered. 'I hope it's not too late, that's all.'

3 9

It was not too late. Not quite. The police
knew what was happening but Tim Bixby's
Commanding Officer did not. The young man
spent nearly two hours trying to convince him
that the double handful of scorched corpses in
his hat were not mice. He would probably
have failed, but at the crucial moment Superintendent Fisk arrived with Doctor Lendall.
Somebody had started a rumour that Britain
was about to suffer a nuclear attack and
there was panic in the town.

Lendall confirmed Tim's story. The Superintendent looked at the C.O. 'We need your
help,' he rapped, 'and quickly. Those creatures
have done something to our radio mast and we
can't co-ordinate our patrols. People are leaving:
loading up their cars and leaving for the open
country. There's a mob outside the Town Hall
screaming about secret shelters. We've tried
telling 'em there are none but it's no use.
They'll storm the place any minute.'

The C.O. acted at once. On his desk sat a red telephone. The town's telephones might be dead, but the trunk-lines between military establishments cannot be broken. He lifted the receiver and spoke rapidly. He didn't say anything about mice. He spoke of civil unrest and the takeover of vital establishments, and when he replaced the instrument he said, 'OK. The procedure's in motion. You can get back into town now. Talk to that mob. Tell them the truth. Say the Forces have the matter in hand.'

By one a.m., units of the armed forces were converging on Market Fulford from every direction. Roadblocks were set up and the flow of traffic ceased. At one-forty, soldiers entered the town's power station. The night-shift, overrun and bitten repeatedly, had fled the premises, but when the soldiers searched the place the mice had slipped away. The troops restored power and threw a cordon round the perimeter.

Three minutes later the telephone exchange was occupied and contact with the outside world resumed.

At one forty-six, troops went into the studios of R.M.F., the local radio station. Moving swiftly they fanned out through the building, kicking in doors. They found the swarm in a store-room and the startled soldiers, who had expected a human adversary, got off several bursts of automatic fire as the creatures scattered.

On a hill outside the town, signallers rigged

up a temporary mast over the twisted remains of the original, and police radios crackled back to life. By two a.m., with all services restored, the town was secure.

On the Tangle, the mice re-grouped. A few bore wounds but most were unscathed. They did not return to the tunnel. There was a disused pipe that ran a quarter of a mile under the town. Deep in its concealing blackness they gathered, to rest and to breed. Soon, they thought, it would be time to try again, but they were wrong. Already, many of them harboured within their bodies another creature: a thing too small to see, which multiplied and spread in the warm damp chamber till all were infected. By the time they realized what was happening, it was too late. They had begun to lose their limbs. Without limbs they could not swarm and without the swarm they had no mind, and so they died. They had journeyed from the region of Betelgeuse in search of a new world, and had succumbed to a brainless organism that is among the smallest in the universe.

40

It was the second day of the spring holidays. It was still early, but already the Tangle was a shimmering green suntrap. Gary Deacon squatted on the parched earth not far from the tunnel, rolling himself a cigarette.

He glanced about, squinting in the glare, and smiled. Except for his two henchmen, Craig and Shaun, he had the place to himself. It shouldn't be long, though, until that cocky Hanley kid showed up. He'd be worse than ever, now that he'd got his name on the telly and his mug in all the papers. Hero of the hour.

Not that Deacon was jealous or anything like that. He had no desire to appear on TV, nor did he want his picture in the press. No. What he wanted was revenge. Revenge for the way the kid had scared him: telling him the coppers were after him. Making him run away and spend two nights in the open. He'd waited a long time to get even with Hanley for that, and today was the day. He ran his tongue along the paper, stuck it down and stood up.

'Come on.' He motioned to the others. 'Inside. He'll be here any minute.' They walked a little way into the tunnel, and leaned against the blackened walls. Deacon lit up and blew out a cloud of smoke. They waited.

Tan ducked through the gap in the fence and waded down through the willow-herb and cow parsley. On the track he turned right and sauntered along with his hands in his pockets. Presently he turned aside and stood, looking down at something in the grass. He was whistling softly to himself and seemed not to notice when three burly figures emerged from the tunnel and strolled towards him.

'Hello, Hanley.'

Tan spun round. His jaw dropped. Deacon grinned.

'What's it like then, being a hero?' he sneered. 'Fed up with it already, are you? Come to get away from all your fans: is that it?'

'No,' replied Tan, quietly. 'That's not it, Deacon. In fact I've brought 'em with me. Look.'

The bully glanced to his left and saw children on the slope: fifteen children, standing among the waist-high weeds, watching him. He turned, and found more children gazing down at him from the other slope. He glared at Tan.

'What is this?' he demanded. 'What're you

trying to pull, Hanley?' Tan stared levelly into his enemy's eyes.

'We're not pulling, Deacon,' he said. 'We're pushing. You. Out. This isn't your territory any more.' He raised his hand. The children started forward, their legs swishing in the long grass. Deacon let out a nervous laugh.

'You're barmy. They're just kids: little kids. Some of 'em are girls.'

'I know,' Tan replied. 'But there are thirty of them, and only one of you. Remember the mice, Deacon?'

'Three!' cried Deacon indignantly. 'There's three of us: or are you blind as well as flippin' daft, Hanley?'

Tan shook his head, praying that things would turn out as Simon had said they would. 'We've got nothing against your mates,' he said. 'They're only rotten because you make 'em rotten, but you were born like that.' He glanced at Craig and Shaun. 'You can go if you want.'

'They're not!' snarled Deacon. 'They're with me.' The henchmen stood confused, looking at the approaching children, then at their leader. Tan jerked his head towards the track. 'Go on. You know you've no chance. He'd run out on you if it was the other way round.'

The youths looked at each other. 'He's right you know,' mumbled Craig. 'He wouldn't stick his neck out for us. Come on.'

He moved past Tan, avoiding Deacon's eyes. Shaun hesitated a moment, then followed. Deacon called after them. 'I won't forget this, Callaghan. And you, Baxter. I'll get you, and when I do you'll be sorry!' He faced Tan with his fists up. 'All right, kid,' he hissed. 'Come and get it.'

It was a brief struggle. The bully's fist made contact with a couple of noses before the children swarmed on him and he was pulled down by sheer weight of numbers to vanish under a pile of those he had terrorized.

'Get his trousers!' cried Tan, and moments later the trousers appeared amid laughter and cheers. Simon held them up, then threw them to Tan. 'Here,' he gasped. 'Let's go!'

Children disentangled themselves from the mêlée and ran away, laughing. Simon dragged his sister clear. There was blood on her lip, but she seemed not to notice. Deacon threshed about under a press of bodies, panting and cursing. The last few children rolled clear and ran, leaving the bully gasping on the ground.

Tan set off up the slope, waving the trousers like a flag. Diane and Simon ran with him. At the top they turned to look back. Deacon stood in his shirt and underpants like a lone gladiator in an empty arena. 'Gimme them pants, Hanley!' he cried, hoarsely.

'We'll leave them in the park,' called Tan. 'On top of the slide: but you'll lose them for good if we catch you on our Tangle again!'

They ducked through the gap and crossed the road. As they did so a car pulled into the kerb. Liz Gordon wound down her window and called to them.

'All right, you three?'

They nodded. 'Yes thanks, Liz.'

'Fine.' She eyed Deacon's trousers. 'What are you up to, Tan?' she asked, suspiciously.

'Me?' said Tan in an innocent voice. 'Nothing. There's this lad, Deacon. He lost his pants and I'm looking after them for him, that's all.'

The reporter smiled. 'You told me Deacon was big, Tan: how did he come to lose his trousers?'

Tan grinned. 'He ran into something bigger,' he said.

THE END

ABOUT THE AUTHOR

Robert Swindells left school at fifteen and worked as a copyholder on a local newspaper. At seventeen he joined the RAF for three years, two of which he served in Germany. He then worked as a clerk, an engineer and a printer before training and working as a teacher. He is now a full-time writer and lives on the Yorkshire moors.

He has written many books for young readers, including many for the Transworld children's lists, his first of which, *Room 13* won the 1990 Children's Book Award, whilst *Abomination* won the 1999 Stockport Children's Book Award and the Sheffield Children's Book Award and was shortlisted for the Whitbread Prize, the Lancashire Children's Book Award *and* the 1999 Children's Book Award. His books for older readers include *Stone Cold*, which won the 1994 Carnegie Medal, as well as the award-winning *Brother in the Land*. As well as writing, Robert Swindells enjoys keeping fit, travelling and reading.

ABOMINATION
Robert Swindells

Martha is twelve, and very different from other kids. No TV. No computer. No cool clothes. Especially no *friends*.
It's all because of her parents. Strict members of a religious group, their rules dominate Martha's life. But one rule is the most important of all: Martha must never *ever* invite anyone home. If she does, their terrible secret – Abomination – could be revealed . . .

'A taut and thrilling novel from a master of the unpredictable'
Daily Telegraph

WINNER OF THE 1999 STOCKPORT
CHILDREN'S BOOK AWARD
WINNER OF THE 1999 SHEFFIELD
CHILDREN'S BOOK AWARD
SHORTLISTED FOR THE WHITBREAD
PRIZE, THE LANCASHIRE CHILDREN'S
BOOK AWARD *and* THE 1999
CHILDREN'S BOOK AWARD

0 440 863627

CORGI YEARLING BOOKS

All Transworld titles are available by post from:

Bookpost, PO Box 29, Douglas, Isle of Man, IM99 1BQ

Credit cards accepted. Please telephone 01624 675137,
fax 01624 670923, Internet http://www.bookpost.co.uk
or e-mail: bookshop@enterprise.net for details

Free postage and packing in the UK. Overseas customers:
allow £1 per book (paperbacks) and £3 per book (hardbacks)